THE BLANK PAGE

THE BLANK PAGE

A Mario Balzic Mystery

K.C. Constantine

MYSTERIOUSPRESS.COM

OPEN ROAD

INTEGRATED MEDIA
NEW YORK

Copyright © 1974 by K.C. Constantine

ISBN: 978-1-5040-9157-2

This edition published in 2024 by MysteriousPress.com/Open Road Integrated Media, Inc.
180 Maiden Lane
New York, NY 10038
www.openroadmedia.com

THE BLANK PAGE

If there was one part of his work that Rocksburg Chief of Police Mario Balzic loathed doing, it was preparing the budget for submission to the city council. If he needed another reason to procrastinate further on it, it was hot. The temperature on Memorial Day had tied a record set in 1910. In the five days since, the forecasts were notable only for their sameness: the temperature was far above the average. There was nothing in the upper air flow, nothing in the ground level patterns out of Canada, no highs to collide with lows coming out of the Gulf of Mexico or South Atlantic to bring rain.

Balzic's mind reeled from the heat and the numbers. He forced himself to check all his calculations twice over, morosely certain that he was making mistakes correcting earlier mistakes. All he could hope was that the council would listen to him for once and allow him to hire an accountant for a couple of weeks the next time a budget was due.

Balzic heard an odd humming about the same time he smelled something burning. He glanced around his tiny office twice before he saw that the oscillating fan atop his file cabinets had quit and was giving off a lazy rope of smoke.

"That caps it," he grumbled, jumping up to shut off the fan.

He stood glowering at the fan for nearly a minute, lamenting silently that on this of all nights, when the temperature was locked in the eighties, his fan had to break. He leaned back across his desk and made a note of it, adding that one to a pile of other notes jumbled in a basket on the corner of his desk marked "Essential." He straightened up with a sigh, took one last glance at the heap of papers on his desk, and went out into the squad room where he saw Desk Sergeant Vic Stramsky nodding off at the radio console.

The hair above Stramsky's ears was slick with perspiration, and Balzic observed with some small malice that the fan near Stramsky's head was still working, though all it seemed to do when its breeze passed over Stramsky was cause his collar points to flutter.

"Vic. Hey Vic!"

Stramsky roused himself. "What's up?"

"I'm going to Muscotti's to get a couple beers. You want me to bring you back one?"

"Nah. It'd just make me sleepier than I am."

The dull chatter of the switchboard sounded, and Stramsky rolled his chair over to plug in the line. He listened for a long moment and then motioned for Balzic to pick up an extension phone.

Balzic heard Stramsky saying, "Yes, ma'am. Would you mind repeating that so I can write it down?"

"All right," the voice said, a voice full of years. "My name is Miss Cynthia Summer. I live at 226 North Hagen Avenue."

"And what's the trouble again, Miss Summer?"

"Well, I hope there isn't any, but something's very odd. You see, I rent rooms to students, ones who attend the community college, don't you see."

"Yes, ma'am."

"And there is one I haven't seen for about two days."

"Maybe he went home for the summer."

"No. That couldn't be. In the first place, it's a she. Janet—oh my, I have to look it up. I have to write everything down. I had a stroke, don't you see, and I just can't remember things the way I used to." There was a pause. "Here it is. Janet Pisula. And she didn't go home for the summer because her classes weren't over until Friday, the twenty-eighth of May. That's today. And then she has final examinations to take, don't you see. All next week."

"Uh, Miss Summer," Stramsky said, "today is the fourth of June."

"It is? Oh my."

"That would mean her classes were over a week ago today, ma'am."

"Well, that makes it even worse, don't you see."

"No, ma'am, I don't."

"Well, young man, if her classes were over last Friday, then she would have had her examinations by now and she would be preparing to move out for the summer, don't you see."

"Uh, Miss Summer, are you sure she didn't leave already?"

"Young man, I do not want to seem impertinent, but I know when my students come and when they go. She didn't leave her key. If she had moved out and I'd forgotten it or didn't notice it, her key would still be here, don't you see. I keep all the keys on a board, right here by the telephone."

"How many students do you have there, Miss Summer?"

"Seven. But I only let six rooms. Two boys are sharing."

"And how many keys do you have there?"

"I have all the keys here."

"What I mean, ma'am, is are we talking about duplicate keys or are we talking about the keys the students themselves had?"

"Why, I have only duplicate keys here, don't you see."

"Then that would mean that none of your students left for the summer."

"Oh my, I'm afraid I don't understand that. But—but that couldn't be, don't you see? Because I have seen all the others."

"Well, ma'am, if you have only the duplicate keys there on your board—"

Balzic interrupted. "Miss Summer, this is Mario Balzic. I'm chief of police here. I've been listening on another phone. Let's just forget about the keys for a minute. Why do you think something's wrong?"

"How do you do," she said. "I've heard a good deal about you."

"Yes, ma'am. Now about this student of yours?"

"Oh. Yes. Well, I haven't seen that girl for, oh my, I thought it was just two days, but if this is the fourth of June, then I haven't seen her for more than a week. And that's just not like her. What I mean to say is that I used to see her every day. We used to chat often. She was a very nice young person. Very lonely, don't you see. But she made a point to stop and chat every day."

"Miss Summer, is it possible you could have seen her and, uh, not remembered? I mean, you said yourself you were having a little trouble remembering things."

The old woman took a moment to reply. When she did, her voice was quivering. "Young man, I did indeed have a stroke, and I do indeed have difficulty remembering things, but I'm not a complete fool."

"Yes, ma'am. I didn't mean for a second you were. But I just thought—never mind. I'll be up to your place in a couple minutes and we'll get this thing straightened out, how's that?"

"Do you think it's necessary for you to come?"

"Well, Miss Summer, we won't know whether it's necessary until we check, now will we?"

"All right. I'll leave the porch light on for you. Oh, what

am I saying—I always leave the porch light on. You'll have to excuse me."

Balzic said good-bye and hung up, looking questioningly at Stramsky.

"Why don't you send somebody else up there?" Stramsky said. "What are you going for?"

"If you think a minute, you'll remember who that old lady is."

"Oh yeah. From the coal family. Summer coal. Yeah, how could I forget that? She gave all that land for the community college."

"That's her. I think she rates a chief. Besides, if I don't go there, I go to Muscotti's, get half drunked up, and then I come back here and make like a bookkeeper—and I can't do that sober."

Balzic headed for the door and went out, letting the screen door bounce against its spring.

Lightning flashed vaguely on the horizon as Balzic got into his cruiser. The lightning was a long way off, and he doubted that a storm would reach Rocksburg—if it ever did—before morning. He turned the cruiser around in the lot and then headed north on Main, thinking it was going to be another miserable night for sleeping.

At the last intersection on Main Street serviced by traffic lights, Balzic turned onto North Hagen Avenue, recollecting the gossip and local lore about the Summer family.

As Rocksburg went, the Summers were as near to aristocracy as the town had ever known. Anybody else who had made money in town, either from the mills or from coal or natural gas, had moved out at the first opportunity. The Summers, for reasons no one bothered to speculate about anymore, had chosen to live where they'd made their fortune.

Clarence Summer had risen from timekeeper through college and law school at night to become attorney for a half-dozen small mines working north of town. Sometime during the three decades from 1890 to 1920, when the steel and coal strikes were at their bloodiest, the mines Summer represented went out of production and into receivership, and when they reopened, by some paper shuffling perhaps only Summer himself understood, they were owned by Clarence Summer.

Sometime in that same period, Summer married. The rumors had been various: he married a Jewess, a Welsh chargirl, a Canadian prostitute. Whatever she had been, she became an alcoholic hermit. Her tastes were odd—gin and beer—and her consumption legendary. The empty bottles that were carted away by garbage collectors were the subject of bets. No one in Rocksburg could say with certainty he had ever heard her first name.

Summer and his wife produced four daughters, and the general opinion was that if Summer was trying to build a dynasty he couldn't have made a worse start. The daughters couldn't wait to escape. Whether they fled from him or from their alcoholic mother or from Rocksburg itself, no one knew. The only one who stayed was the one everyone—including herself—called Miss Cynthia, the first born, the only one who never married.

For years, well into the late 1950s, Miss Cynthia sustained her wealth and her remoteness. Then, bit by piece, things began to slip away. The mines veined out. Where once there had been four main shafts, each bearing the name of a daughter and the number of the order of her birth—Cynthia Number One, Edna Number Two, Elaine Number Three, and Roseann Number Four—each employing nearly a hundred miners, by 1960 all four shafts had been sealed on orders of the state bureau of mines to prevent the possibility of surface air feeding a fire that had begun in a shaft owned by another company but which came very near Elaine Number Three.

Clarence's wife died in the last great diphtheria epidemic in the thirties. Clarence himself lost to cancer in the early forties. The other daughters, Edna, Elaine, and Roseann, appeared only as names and faces on the society pages of the Pittsburgh newspapers and then, one by one, on the obituary pages. Miss Cynthia clung to the house and life.

The chauffeur went first. Then the gardener, the maids, and the cook. The Lincoln Continental went soon after the chauffeur. The rock gardens, the rose gardens, the hedge gardens with the fountains and the sundials began to look like parodies of themselves.

Miss Cynthia shopped for herself; she could not even command a taxi to wait until she finished. When she entered the supermarkets, she clutched a sheaf of coupons Cut from *The Rocksburg Gazette* offering discounts on certain products, and when she left and waited for another taxi to pick her up, she tried not to lean on a shopping cart in which a solitary bag was filled mostly with frozen dinners.

Sometime in the mid-sixties, she made an arrangement with the Conemaugh County commissioners for the land behind the house. The commissioners had been planning for some time to begin a community college, but were stymied by the price of land at a time when they'd been advised the bond market was unfavorable. Miss Cynthia, it was said around city hall and in the county court house, offered the forty acres behind her house in return for an exemption from real estate and school taxes on the house in which she insisted she was going to live until she died. It was also said that the house would at her death automatically become county property with the provision that it become part of the community college and be named Clarence Summer Hall.

In 1968, when the first college building was completed on

her land—a combination of classrooms, library, and student union—Miss Cynthia's financial desperation became clear: she placed an ad in *The Rocksburg Gazette* welcoming students to lease rooms from her at the incredible rate of twelve dollars a month; this, when a single room with bath in Rocksburg was going for a minimum of fifty dollars a month.

Balzic approached the house now, once an imposing and impeccable two-story red brick structure said to have six bathrooms, over a pitted asphalt drive leading to the front portico. Two faded white columns supported a weather roof over the drive. As Miss Cynthia had said, the portico light was on, but only one light of the two still burned. When Balzic knocked, he saw that the other lamp no longer had a bulb in it.

Miss Cynthia answered the door herself. Her left eye was half closed and her left cheek sagged, drawing down the corner of her mouth. She was disconcertingly thin, and her left arm dangled lifelessly.

"Miss Summer," Balzic said, holding out his ID case. "I'm Mario Balzic."

"Please come in, Chief Balzic." She tried to smile. "I can't tell you how sorry I am to have to meet you like this." It was an effort for her to close the door. "You'll want the key, won't you?"

"Yes, ma'am," Balzic said, following her across the foyer, noticing with a vague remorse the difficulty with which she walked, her left shoe never leaving the floor but sliding along. She led him to a telephone under a stairway. Balzic was not surprised to see that it was a pay phone.

Miss Cynthia took a key off a square board by the phone and handed it to Balzic. "Her room is the last one on the right upstairs. I'm sorry I can't take you up. Those stairs are just impossible for me these days. I really hope . . ."

16

"We'll see, Miss Summer. But first we have to look."

He took the stairs slowly, observing the house as he went. It was more generally deteriorated than he'd expected, and he had the feeling of being in a house just a signature away from a sheriff's sale.

At the top of the stairs he oriented himself. There were two halls: one led straight ahead of the stairs, the other began about ten feet back from the stairs and led to the left. Balzic went straight ahead to the last door on the right.

He could hear voices in the room opposite, young male voices involved in what sounded like a mild argument over a problem in mathematics.

Balzic had trouble with the lock. It seemed a fairly new lock and the edges of the key were still sharp. It took Balzic a moment to realize that rather than opening the door he had done the opposite. He repeated his motions with the key and was certain when he finally pushed open the door that it had been unlocked when he first inserted the key.

Inside the room, a gooseneck lamp was burning on a tiny desk against the far wall. Balzic noticed that first. Then the smell hit him and he saw the rest and nearly gagged.

She was on her back on the floor beside the bed and naked except for her panties. Twisted around her neck was another undergarment, a slip or a brassiere perhaps, but Balzic did not want to get close enough to look. Her features were horribly distorted from the swelling, and her flesh from her neck to her hairline was the color of a week-old bruise. On her stomach was a plain white sheet of paper. As far as Balzic could tell there was nothing written on it, but he couldn't bring himself to reach down and pick it up.

Something kept wanting to come up in Balzic's throat. He had to force himself to look at her. Her body was slender, boyish almost, with small breasts, and she did not appear to Balzic to be much taller than his eldest daughter. He swept his gaze around the room long enough to notice that there was no particular disarray, then he backed out, locked the door, and hurried down the stairs to the phone,

As he was dialing, he heard Miss Cynthia ask him if everything was all right.

"No, ma'am, it isn't."

"Oh my," she said.

"Rocksburg Police, Sergeant Stramsky speaking."

"Vic. Mario. Get the D.A., the coroner, and the state boys. We got a homicide at 226 North Hagen Avenue. I'll be waiting out front for them."

"Got it," Stramsky replied, and the phone went dead. Balzic hung up and saw Miss Cynthia. He reached out and touched her on the shoulder.

"Oh my," she said. "Oh my . . ."

The state police Criminal Investigation Division squad, under the temporary command of Lt. Walker Johnson, arrived first. Much to Balzic's spiteful pleasure Johnson had been transferred from Erie to replace Lt. Harry Minyon while Minyon rode out about with his ulcers in Conemaugh General Hospital. Any replacement for Minyon would have pleased Balzic, but Johnson was especially welcome to him as their friendship went back to days when Balzic had first made chief and Johnson was a sergeant on the narcotics squad. Two nights ago, on Johnson's first night back in Rocksburg, the two of them had gotten pleasantly drunk on Balzic's back porch, regaling each other with decade-old anecdotes. . . .

Johnson came downstairs after he'd put his squad to work and waited for Balzic to introduce Miss Cynthia. A moment after the introduction, Johnson nodded to Balzic and led the way out to the foyer near the front door.

"This is a hell of a way to start," Johnson said.

"Well, at least it won't be dull."

"Yeah. It won't be that. So, old buddy, what do you have?"

"Next to nothing. The lady had a stroke—which you noticed—and I don't know what we're going to get out of her. She thought today was the twenty-eighth of May."

"How about the two kids in the room across the hall—you talk to them yet?"

"I'll tell you what, Walk. I damn near got sick up there. That girl's not much bigger than my Marie. Older, I'm sure, but not any bigger. It just got to, me, so I just locked up and came down and called you."

"Say nothing. I couldn't stand it myself. By now every one of those poor bastards up there'll have a hanky in his mouth." Johnson thought for a moment. "Is Grimes still coroner here?"

"Yeah. He should've been here by now. The D.A., too."

Johnson shrugged. "You want to stay with the lady? Or you want the two kids upstairs?"

"I better stick with her. She's supposed to have four or five more roomers in here, you know."

"Wonder where they are. They live here, they can't be locals. This is a hell of a time. School year's damn near over. They're all students, aren't they?"

Balzic nodded.

"I hope to hell they haven't left for home," Johnson said. "If they have, we'll be chasing all over hell." He shrugged again and went back upstairs.

Balzic went back into what had once been the living room where he found Miss Cynthia sitting listlessly on the corner of a worn and faded maroon velvet couch.

He sat beside her. "Miss Summer, I'm going to have to ask you some questions, so is there anything I can get you before we get started?"

"No, thank you. You're kind to think of it, but no. I'm just worried that I won't be able to help, and . . ."

"And what?"

"Well, all these police. Is it really, I mean—"

"I'm afraid so, Miss Summer. The girl—well, didn't you hear me when I was talking on the phone?"

"Yes," Miss Cynthia said slowly. "Yes, I heard you. I suppose I didn't want to believe it." Her mottled hand went to her papery lips. "She was such a lovely person. But so lonely."

"How so?"

"She was an orphan. She was raised by an aunt and uncle. That much I remember, but for the life of me, I can't think where. I have it written down. I can get the address for you."

"Not right now. Later on you'll have to give me the names and addresses of all your roomers. But for now, let's just talk about what you remember about her."

"What I remember—oh my. I don't even remember very clearly when I last talked to her. I thought it was three days ago. Now, I'm just not sure."

"Well tell me what you are sure of."

"I'm sure that she had no parents or brothers or sisters. I'm sure she was kind. Practically the first thing she said after she said hello was to ask if there was anything she could get me. Why, that first week I was home from the hospital after my stroke, she stayed down here with me all night, don't you see. I never asked her to, but when I'd wake during the night, she'd be asleep in a chair near my bed. We had even discussed the possibility of her living down here with me next year as a sort of, oh you know, a sort of companion to me."

"She must have had friends," Balzic said.

"I really can't say. I don't know how she got along with my other students. She never discussed them with me—or if she did I just don't remember."

"Do you remember anyone visiting her?"

"No. I can't say for certain. She may have. The students are always coming and going. I can't say if anyone was coming to see her. I just have this impression that no one did. I can't say why."

"Did she have dates?"

"I don't think so. We talked about that occasionally. I used to tell her that youth was not to be squandered, things like that. Things old people try to tell young people. But it struck me that she really wasn't aware that she was a woman. She could have been very attractive, but she seemed not to know how to make herself attractive. She had a rather plain face, and it seemed she didn't know anything about cosmetics. She had a lovely, slim figure, but she didn't think about clothes at all."

Balzic nodded. "Do you remember hearing anything unusual?"

"No. I'm sorry. I just missed seeing her. That's why I called you. But I don't recall any noises, anything out of the ordinary. But you must understand, chief, this stroke has also left me deaf in my left ear. You have a very powerful voice. Very resonant. It's easy enough to hear you. But much goes on that I don't hear. I suppose for that reason I make a very accommodating land-lady for my students. Their music—well, all I hear is a rhythmic thumping. I would dearly like to hear it, but . . ."

"Did she ever speak to you about any trouble?"

"No. She wasn't rich, heaven knows. But she had been cared for, some sort of trust fund. She told me about it once, but I don't remember any details. I don't think she was having any difficulty with the relatives who raised her. At least I don't recall her speaking about anything like that."

"Didn't she ever talk about anything that was bothering her? There must have been something."

"The only thing I remember like that was something about a course she was having problems with. A composition course I believe it was. For a time she was bewildered by it all. I recall her saying once that she didn't know what that man wants, something like that. But that was some time ago. In the winter. December or January, I think. Of course, you must consider my sense of time these days."

"That was the only thing?"

"I'm sorry, chief. You must understand. That's all I can remember."

Balzic stood. "Miss Summer, I'll have to see your records now. The students' names, home addresses, how they stood with the rent."

"I'll get that for you. I keep it all locked in my desk in the kitchen. I can tell you now that all of my students were very prompt about the rent."

Balzic helped her up and then followed her into the kitchen. He had just finished copying the names and addresses from her ledger when Dr. Wallace Grimes, the county coroner, appeared in the foyer. He was still wearing his suit coat and his tie was knotted tightly. He wiped his forehead with a folded hanky and replaced it carefully in his breast pocket, nodding to Balzic and saying, "Mario," by way of greeting and asking at the same time where he was to find his work.

"Upstairs, doc," Balzic said.

Grimes went up without a word, and a moment or two later Johnson came down. Balzic met him at the foot of the stairs.

"What did you get, Mario?"

"Not much. Names and addresses of the other students. Nobody owed. The lady's hearing is bad and her memory's about the same. The only thing she could say for sure was that the girl was an orphan. No brothers, no sisters. Raised by an aunt and uncle. The only thing she thought might have been bothering the girl was some trouble in her classwork. A composition course. But she thought that was around last December or January. She couldn't remember hearing anything more about it since. What did you get?"

"The two kids are a blank," Johnson said. "All they remember is seeing her once in a while. They didn't even miss her. One of them thought he heard something funny about a week ago, but he didn't think anything more about it. The other one thought he saw a guy standing in front of her door a couple of weeks ago, but then when he thought about it he couldn't say whether the guy was standing in front of her door or was just standing in the hall. He says he never saw the guy before or since. Couldn't give me the vaguest make. Had no idea whether the guy was old or young, tall, short, nothing. All he said for sure was the guy was white. And then he started to think about that."

"Your people come up with anything?"

"Well, who knows what was there? But there's plenty of money still around. For a college kid, I mean. Twenty-five-something in bills and change in her desk drawer, another couple bucks in bills and change in her wallet. Nothing was knocked over. The rest of her clothes were on the foot of the bed, laid out neat, like she was just undressing and hadn't thought to hang anything on hangers.

"Just as a first guess," Johnson went on, "I'd say somebody either talked her into getting undressed and when she got that far he just slipped the brassiere around her neck and strangled her with it. Either that or else he walked in on her when she had got down to just those two pieces of clothing. Either she knew him or else he caught her completely by surprise because the two across the hall definitely did not hear anything resembling a scream or a yell for help. And they also claim they've both been in their room every day and night for the past two weeks except to go to classes and to eat. They both say they're too broke to do anything else."

"You don't think them?"

"Who knows? But right now, they just look too goddamn goggle-eyed. You know the look. Couple of squares. They got all this information to volunteer, they want to say all this stuff to help, but it all comes out a lot of words."

"What do you make of the paper?"

Johnson gave a barely audible snort. "That's the goddamndest thing I've ever seen. The guy that did it had to put it there, but why?"

"Nothing on it?"

"Not a damn thing. Unless you count the smudge of a print. Just a piece of white typing paper."

"More like it in the room?" Balzic said.

"Yeah. About half a ream by the typewriter on the desk. Same stuff."

"Anything else?"

"I looked at her fingernails. I got a man scraping them, but I have the feeling he's not going to find a thing. I couldn't see anything myself. Not even a crack in one of them. Like she didn't put up any resistance at all."

"Maybe she was surprised."

"Sure, there's that possibility. But you'd think she'd have made some attempt to save her life. I mean, what the hell, Mario? Even if she was grabbed from behind, caught completely unaware, you'd think she would've dug her nails into something. Her own throat, something, just trying to get that thing off her neck. Nobody loses consciousness that fast. But nothing—unless it's something that has to go under a scope. But that paper. Wow..."

Dr. Grimes came down the steps then, buttoning his collar and running up his tie.

"What's the word, doc?" Balzic said.

"That should have been obvious," Grimes said evenly. "Suffocation caused by strangulation. Six, seven, maybe eight days ago. Give me some time and I'll get it down to the day. What's keeping the ambulance people—or did somebody not think to call?"

"They should have been here long ago," Balzic said. "I'll get on them."

"Tell them to go right to the hospital morgue," Grimes said, going for the door. "I'll be waiting for them. Good night."

Balzic called Stramsky to hurry the ambulance and learned that every available one was on a call. "Couple heart attacks and a four-car pile-up coming out of Conemaugh Shopping Center. Nothing serious, but every car had a family in it," Stramsky said. Balzic grunted and then hung up. He went back to tell Johnson and saw him talking to a plump, barefoot girl who kept peeking around Johnson's shoulders, darting glances at the officers coming and going on the stairs.

Johnson introduced the girl—Evelyn Embry—to Balzic. She had a pleasant enough face, softened by its roundness, but her reticence in answering Johnson's questions had an edge of arrogance about it that Balzic found immediately disagreeable. In spite of himself, Balzic kept glancing at the girl's feet and the dirt caked between her toes.

". . . so you didn't know her very well," Johnson was saying.

"Yeah, uh, I mean I talked to her, you know, but that's all."

"Do you recall the last time you saw her?"

"Uh-uh. Couple days ago, I guess."

"She's been dead longer than that."

"Oh. Well—I don't know. Maybe a week ago."

"Did you ever see anybody with her?"

"No. But like I said, I really didn't know. I mean, I didn't see her that much. I only talked to her a couple times." She thought for a moment. "Does this, uh, mean I have to stay around? I mean, I am getting ready to leave. I'm all packed and everything."

"Stay around for what?" Johnson asked.

"Oh, you know—I don't know," she said, giggling nervously. "Don't you guys always make the witnesses stay around or something?"

Johnson shot a wearied glance at Balzic who, again in spite of himself, was looking at the girl's filthy feet. "No, Miss Embry. We have your home address if you want to leave. If we need to talk to you again, we'll get in touch with your parents."

"Oh, I'm not going home."

"Well, your family will know where you'll be, won't they?"

"I hope not."

"Uh, Miss Embry, it's not likely that we'll need to talk to you again, but just in case, you better let your family know where you're going to be. You can go now. Just please stay out of the way upstairs, okay?"

Johnson shook his head at Balzic as the girl went up the steps.

"You know," Balzic said, "I was talking to a chemist a couple weeks ago. If these barefoot kids only knew how much crap they walked through in a day. . . ."

The ambulance came and left, the attendants soaked with perspiration by the time they got the stretcher to the bottom of the stairs.

District Attorney Milt Weigh stopped on his way home from a county Democrat meeting, staying only long enough to make general inquiries and to offer the services of his squad of detectives.

"He looked like the Democrats are serving better booze than they used to," Johnson said after Weigh had gone.

Balzic smiled weakly, feeling too hot to make a rejoinder. "Think your boys came up with anything yet?"

"About time I checked," Johnson said, going slowly up the steps.

Balzic walked through the foyer to the front door, catching sight of Miss Summer sitting on the worn velvet couch, fanning herself with an envelope. He stepped out onto the portico and scanned the horizon looking for lightning. When it flashed, it seemed even duller and more distant than it had earlier.

He smoked and thought about that single sheet of paper on the girl's stomach and then about the girl and then about his own daughter, Marie. His thoughts were a jumble. Nothing made sense. He felt the way he felt when he read a newspaper account of some seemingly isolated act of violence, when the reporter called the act "senseless." The word annoyed and angered him because he believed that no violence was truly senseless. It always made sense if you took the time to analyze it. He believed that was as true about the violence done upstairs as about any other violence he had known, except that everything about this violence did indeed appear senseless. There had been no robbery, no sound, no struggle, and he was willing to bet that there had been no sex. He would have to wait for the coroner's report to be certain of that, but, without being able to explain or justify his feeling to himself, he was sure sex had had no part in what had happened to this orphan, this Janet Pisula. He was as sure of that as he was unsure what the piece of paper on her stomach meant. There was a message there, but one without words and one that therefore said everything at the same time it said nothing.

Balzic flipped his cigarette butt into the night and went back inside just as Johnson was coming down the stairs.

"Anything?" Balzic said.

"About a thousand prints up there. Naturally, the ones we'd like to have—off that paper—we're not going to get. Whoever it was probably licked his index finger and just got enough of his index finger and thumb to lift it and put it on her. We'll have to send it to the FBI lab anyway to make sure. They're the only ones with the equipment to get a print off paper, but my man says they're not going to be able to do anything with what's there." Johnson scratched his chin. "Mario, tell me again how the room was when you went in."

"The door was unlocked, I'm certain of that. The desk lamp was on, nothing was knocked around. That's about all I really noticed. The smell got to me and I had to get the hell out."

"How do you figure that?" Johnson said. "In this heat—God. You'd've thought somebody would've smelled it before this. They all had to come down these steps. Her door's not fifteen feet away from the top."

"I didn't get it until I opened the door, if that's any help. Do you remember when it first hit you?"

"Now that you mention it, no," Johnson said. "But it doesn't make sense. It goes against all the laws of the nose." He looked thoughtfully at the floor. "Where the hell are the rest of them? How many are there again, total?"

"Seven. We've seen four. That leaves three."

"Male or female?"

"Two females, one male."

"And they're all still here? None left for the summer?"

"According to Miss Summer and to the keys on her board, they should all be here."

"Did you try to get the next of kin?"

"Not yet. But I hate like hell to tell anybody that over the phone. And that's a long drive down there. Thirty-five, forty miles. Why don't you see if you've got some people in the vicinity?"

"I suppose I better," Johnson said.

Balzic handed him the address of Mr. and Mrs. Michael Pisula, and Johnson went outside to his cruiser to make the call to the barracks to have the detail assigned. He returned in a few minutes and said, "We got some people in the area. They'll handle it."

"A piece of paper," Balzic said, shaking his head. "One piece of blank typing paper . . ."

They were standing there, smiling absurdly at one another when the front door opened and two girls came timidly into the foyer. The first was very tall, very slim, dressed in faded jeans, a sleeveless cotton jersey, and sandals. The other, shorter but equally slim, also wore jeans and sandals with a man's tee-shirt which had been dyed a myriad of pastel colors. Both carried books and notebooks and had similar shoulder bags made of fringed suede.

Johnson introduced himself and Balzic to the girls.

"Which one of you is Kimberly Marsinsky?" Balzic asked.

"I am," the taller one said, flushing.

"And you're Patricia Kein?" Balzic said to the other.

"Keim," she corrected him.

"What's the matter?" Kimberly asked. "What happened—I mean, what's going on?"

"One of your fellow tenants is dead," Johnson said. "Janet Pisula."

"Janet who?" Patricia asked.

"I never heard of her," Kimberly said. The girls looked at each other quizzically.

"She lived in the room at the top of the stairs. On the right."

"Oh. Her," Patricia said.

"Why do you say it like that?" Johnson said.

"Well, I didn't mean it to sound like it sounded—I guess. It's just, well, I don't know. But if you're here, then . . ."

"I'll save the speculation," Johnson said. "She was murdered."

Both girls sucked in their breath. "Oh my God," Kimberly said. "When—how—you mean right here?"

"Right here. In her room. We know how, but we don't know when exactly. We were hoping you could help us with that."

"I didn't even know her," Kimberly said. "I never even talked to her. I didn't—I'll bet I didn't see her four or five times. And every time I saw her, she was in there talking with the old lady."

"You knew her, Patricia," Johnson said.

"I didn't *know* her. I talked to her twice. Once for about fifteen minutes over in the Union. She wanted to know about an assignment we had in comp. The other time was outside the library about, oh, three or four weeks ago. We talked for about a half-hour or so."

"Why did you say, 'Oh, her,' the way you said it? Before, I mean, when we told you who it was."

"I don't know. I guess because she impressed me as being a very unaware person."

"Unaware in what way?"

"I don't know. It's hard to say why you think somebody is aware and why somebody else isn't. Awareness is a difficult thing to define."

"Well try," Balzic said. "We have to have some idea what you're talking about."

"She was just out of it, that's all."

Johnson scratched his neck and glared at the wall beyond Balzic's shoulder. Balzic let out a heavy sigh and said, "Look, Patricia—"

"Please don't call me that. Just Pat, okay? I hate Patricia."

"Okay, Pat. But look. I've got two daughters, and I know

what it is to try and understand them when they start using their slang, and I'm aware—huh?—aware that slang changes pretty fast. The point I'm trying to make is you got to put your impressions and feelings about this girl into something specific, something solid that a couple foggy bottoms like the lieutenant here and me can understand. Saying she was a 'very unaware person' or 'out of it'—that tells us nothing. Because I'll tell you something she was and is for a plain fact. She was a victim. She is now a corpse. And whoever victimized her and turned her into a corpse—no matter how out of it you thought she was— that somebody did it right here. Where *you* live. And there is nothing we know now to guarantee us or you that he doesn't have it in his head to turn some other young girl into a corpse. Is that plain enough for you?"

"Oh wow," Kimberly said.

"That's plain enough," Pat said. "I'm sorry. I'll try."

"Good," Balzic said. "Now let's start with the first time you talked to her. What was that about?"

"Well, that's funny—I mean, obviously it isn't funny. It's ironic though, because the first time I talked to her was last semester. About the second week. We were in the same comp class, and the assignment was to define an abstraction as concretely as we could. And I remember telling her almost exactly what you just told me, I mean, I told her she had to be as specific as she could. I tried to tell her to take as simple an abstraction as she could think of, something very elemental like a season of the year and just make a list of all the things she could think of when that word came into her head. But she didn't even have the awareness that a season of the year was an abstraction."

"And that's all you talked about? Nothing else?"

The Keim girl nodded.

"What about the second time, by the library I think you said."

She nodded. "Well, that time she stopped me and said she had to talk to somebody about something very important but she didn't know who to talk to. And then she said something—I couldn't help it—when she said it, I just started laughing at her. Oh, wow, what a bummer for her."

"What did she say?"

"Oh wow, she said she'd always admired me. It was the way she said admired. So worshippy, God, it was like she should have been lighting a candle or something."

"Go on," Johnson said.

"Well, she got so embarrassed, she just turned crimson. I've never seen anybody blush like that in my life. And then she started talking real fast and it was all about comp again, but I could see right away that wasn't what she really wanted to talk about and that she was just making that up as she went because she didn't know how to get out of talking to me."

"So," Balzic said, running his tongue over a molar, "you got the impression—well, let me ask you. Did she talk about anything else?"

"No. And after a couple more minutes, she started blushing again and said she had to go someplace, and then she practically ran away from me."

"Let me get something else straight," Balzic said. "You were both in the same composition class the first semester. Were you still in the same class this semester?"

"No. She couldn't get along with Keenan at all. She used to catch a lot of flak from him. So did everybody, really. But everybody gave it back to him. Except her. And I really gave it back to him. I guess maybe that's why she said she admired me. I couldn't think of any other reason. I never saw her anyplace else. Just class and here. But I never talked to her here. Just to say hello."

"Keenan was the teacher?"

"He's also chairman of the department. And the only one with a doctorate. The others, Winoski and Farrell, they just have their master's."

"Don't forget Snavely," Kimberly said.

"That toad," Pat said.

"I don't think he even has a bachelor's," Kimberly said.

"Who did Janet have for composition this semester?" Balzic asked.

"Farrell, I think," Pat said. "I'm not sure. She told me that time outside the library, but I forgot."

"Do you know, Kimberly?"

"No, I don't."

"Okay, let's forget about teachers for a while. What about the last couple weeks? When was the last time either of you saw this girl? And please think carefully."

"The last time I saw her was a couple weeks ago," Kimberly said. "She was in there talking to the old lady."

"Pat?"

"A week, maybe ten days ago. She was just going into her room and I was coming up the steps. I didn't talk to her though."

"Ever see anybody going into her room or standing outside her door or knocking on her door or coming out of her room?"

Both girls shook their heads.

"Did you hear anything or see anything out of the ordinary in the last week or so—anything at all?"

Again, the same negative response.

"What the hell," Balzic said under his breath, half turning away from the girls and speaking softly to Johnson. "A girl lives here since when—last September? Six other people pass fifteen feet from her door every time they go out or come in and nobody knows a goddamn thing about her. You tell me, Walk."

Johnson shrugged and scratched his neck. "Listen, girls, thank you very much for your cooperation. There's just one more thing. Let whoever you live with know where you're going to be. If we want to ask you anything else, we'll get in touch with you. We have your home addresses. You can go now. And thanks again."

The girls apologized for not being able to help much, then went up the stairs to their rooms, leaving Balzic and Johnson once again to stare at each other and shake their heads foolishly.

"Who's left?" Johnson asked.

"Uh, one Nicholas Cerovich," Balzic said, reading from the list he had copied from Miss Summer's ledger.

"What do you bet he knows as much as the rest of them?"

"No bet," Balzic said, going into the living room to ask Miss Summer if she knew anything about him.

"Cerovich," she said slowly. "Oh, yes. Nicholas. He's working. He won't be here until after midnight."

"Do you know where he works?"

"You'll have to give me a moment, chief. It's here in Rocksburg, that much I know. I'll think of the place." She frowned and closed her eyes as though trying to visualize the name of the place.

"Is it one of the mills?"

"It's a mill, but give me another word for a mill and I might be able to think of it."

"Uh, factory, fabricating plant, foundry, forge—"

"That's it. Forge. He works at a forge."

"Fort Pitt Chain and Forge?"

"Yes. That's it."

"Thank you, Miss Summer," Balzic said, going to the phone and rooting through his pockets for a dime. "I located him," he said to Johnson. "You got any dimes?" he said, flipping through the pages of the directory. Johnson handed him some dimes just as Balzic found the number. He dialed, identifying himself when he got an answer, and asked for someone familiar with the names of employees. "Just a routine verification that a man is employed there, that's all."

"I'm only a security guard, chief," the voice replied. "There's nobody here in any of the offices."

"What's working now?"

"Just the forge crew. Plus some guys on the loading dock."

"The name Cerovich mean anything to you—Nicholas Cerovich?"

"Oh yeah, sure. The college kid. Yeah, he's here. He's down with the labor gang in the forge. You want to talk to him?"

"No. I'll tell you what. Let me talk to his boss."

"Sure, sure. Hold on." There was a click, a buzz, then a ringing.

"Forge. Sokolosky," a voice shouted over the roar of the furnaces and the thunderous slamming of forge hammers.

"This is Chief of Police Balzic," he said, holding the phone away from his ear. "I'm just trying to verify that you have a Nicholas Cerovich working for you. Is he there now?"

"Yeah. You wanna talk to him?"

"No. Just tell me what shift he works and whether he misses work."

"He works steady second trick. He don't miss any work. Hasn't missed a day since he started. He's a good kid. Helluva worker."

"When did he start?"

"Four o'clock like everybody else."

"No, no. I mean, when'd he start working there?"

"Oh. Last summer. June I think. Been about a year now."

"Have you been his boss all this time?"

"I been everybody's boss on second trick for eleven years."

"And he hasn't missed any work at all? Especially in the last couple weeks?"

"Hey, look. Maybe you ought to talk to him. I don't like this talking about somebody that works for me with a cop. If he did something wrong, you come talk to him."

"I don't need to talk to him. All I want from you is your word that he hasn't missed work, that's all."

"Well you got it, brother. Not only don't he miss work, the sonuvabrick is always yapping can he get some overtime. Is 'at what you wanna hear?"

"That's good enough," Balzic said. "And thanks for your help."

"Yeah, sure. Anytime. Just remember me the next time my old lady gets a ticket. Joe Sokolosky. See you around, chief." The phone clicked, and Balzic was laughing as he hung up.

"So?" Johnson said.

"So, Nicholas Cerovich works steady second trick at Fort Pitt Chain and Forge, he's been working for almost a year, and he hasn't missed a day. Which means he probably knows as little as the rest."

"Oh boy," Johnson said. "You know what that means."

"Yeah," Balzic said. "I wonder how many people there are tied up with this damn college."

"Well, how about you finding out, okay? I'll hang in here until we run everything down or pick everything up. I also want to talk to those two across the hall from her room again. They might've remembered something; I might've forgot to ask them something. See how many names you can get, and then we'll see how we divide the labor. We'll probably have to use the D.A.'s people . . . you got somebody you can call?"

"I can start with the president of the college," Balzic said. "I met him last year at some banquet or other."

"Well, he's all yours," Johnson said, starting up the stairs again and muttering something about the heat while Balzic thumbed through the phone directory looking for the home address of Dr. J. Hale Beverley, president of Conemaugh County Community College.

Dr. J. Hale Beverley lived in the Crestmont Plan, a post-Korean War development known among Rocksburg's blue collars as Pill Hill. As a hill it didn't seem much, a gentle rise of ground on the northeastern edge of Rocksburg, but from its crest on clear days when there was no suggestion of a temperature inversion, all of Rocksburg was visible beneath it. As for the pills, most of the staff of Conemaugh General Hospital lived there, plus the majority of specialists, generalists, and dentists who kept at least one office in Rocksburg or its environs. Lately, some lawyers had moved to its fringes, and here and there an engineer had crept in, but among the thirty-five or forty houses clustered on the slopes there was not one chiropractor, mortician, minister, insurance agent, or automobile dealer. How Dr. J. Hale Beverley had managed to find entrance piqued Balzic's curiosity. Either realtors were becoming more democratic or else they didn't know one doctor from another.

Balzic counted fifteen cars either in or near the driveway to the Beverleys' two-car garage, and he knew he was going to have to interrupt a party, most likely the year-end bash a college president was expected to throw for his faculty and staff.

As Balzic pushed the button and listened to the two-toned chimes, he caught the sound of a stereo, and when the door opened, a tall, stiffly erect man with a wispy reddish mustache and beard stood in the door frame. He had a nearly empty tumbler in his hand and a tipsily foolish grin on his face.

"Welcome," he said. "Come and join us. Don't tell the host, of course. I was just on my way to the ice and thought I'd stop and invite you."

"Uh-huh," Balzic said, taking out his ID and holding it up. "I'm here to see Dr. Beverley. I called about five minutes ago and talked to Mrs. Beverley, I think. She said she'd tell her husband I was on the way, but maybe you could tell him I'm here—on your way back from the ice."

"Of course. I'll be more than happy to tell him. But why don't you step in and have a drink while you're waiting?"

"No, thanks. Just give him the message."

"Who is it, Mal?" asked a woman, coming up behind the man.

"The fuzzzzzz," Mal said, holding his finger up to his lips in a hokey gesture to be cautious, spilling in the process the last drops from his glass on the lapel of his corduroy jacket. "Whoopsey," he said. Then he abruptly shifted the glass to his left hand and thrust out his right at Balzic. "Forgot my manners," he said. "Malcolm Keenan here. I'm a poet who teaches as a public service."

Balzic took the hand and felt the shaking up to his shoulder.

"Your name again, sir?" Keenan said.

"Balzic."

"Ballsy did you say? I remember a limerick which goes, let me see now—ah, yessss. 'There was a man from Boston, who had a little red Austin; there was room for his ass, and a gallon of gas, but his—'"

"Mal, for god's sake, you're not going to start with those awful things again, are you?" the woman said. She put her hands on Keenan's shoulders and gently began to turn him around and away from the door. "To the kitchen with you," she said.

"'—but his balls hung out and he lost 'em,'" Keenan said, grinning over his shoulder as he submitted to her pushing.

"Don't mind him," the woman said. "Now. What can I do for you?"

Balzic held up his ID again and said, "I called a few minutes ago—"

"Oh yes," she said, studying the ID while Balzic studied her. She was young, thirty at most, with a rather ordinary face that was meticulously made up, and her black dress had what struck Balzic as an improbable combination of propriety and allure about it which he imagined she must have spent some time trying to find. It was unadorned, buttoned to the neck, sleeveless, but made of a material which clung to her more than ample figure.

"Well, I must apologize," she said. "I'm the person to whom you spoke on the phone. I'm Mrs. Beverley, but I'm afraid I haven't had a chance to tell him that you want to see him. Why don't you come in while I do that?"

"Fine."

"I imagine you'll want to be alone," Mrs. Beverley said, "so why don't you just go into the den? Right through that door." She pointed to a door down a short hall. "Right next to the john," she said, turning back into the large living room on the right.

Balzic paused in the opening to the living room on his way to the den. He saw at least twenty-five people, the men dressed for the most part informally, the women wearing a variety of styles. One rather blocky woman wore short denim culottes, flat-heeled sandals, and a blue tee-shirt upon which were painted the words "POT POWER" above a crude outline of a toilet. Another wore a long-sleeved white blouse buttoned to the neck and a red satiny skirt that nearly touched the floor but was split halfway up her thighs. Still another wore silver backless pumps, an extremely short silver lamé dress to show off her very good, very long legs, and clutched a silver bag like a shield to her chest.

They all turned to look at Balzic as Mrs. Beverley approached someone just out of Balzic's view and announced, "The chief of police is here, Jay Hale, and he wants to see you."

Balzic waited a moment longer to see their reaction. It was mostly curiosity he observed, except for the blocky woman in the tee-shirt who went immediately to the stereo and turned up the volume on a rock song and began a provocative dance which belied her construction. After she was sure Balzic was watching her, she danced her way to a squatting, bullishly built young man who looked familiar to Balzic, pulled him to his feet, and continued her dance with him, looking then straight into Balzic's eyes.

Balzic couldn't resist. Before he stepped out of the doorway, he blew the blocky dancer a kiss. It stopped her cold, and then she threw back her head and shook with laughter.

Balzic found the john and was about to open the next door when Keenan reappeared, his glass a deep amber color with only one ice cube in it. "Say," Keenan said, "have you heard the one that goes, 'There was a young lady named Alice, who peed in a Catholic chalice; 'twas done out of need, the bishop agreed, and not out of Protestant malice'—have you heard that one?"

"I just did," Balzic said, smiling.

"Oh," Keenan said. "Too bad. It's one of my favorites." He weaved around Balzic and headed back toward the living room, stumbling once on a deep-pile throw rug.

"Oh boy," Balzic said, going into the den and switching on a desk lamp. "So that's Keenan."

He recalled what Patricia Keim had said about Keenan: chairman of the English department and the only Ph.D. And how had he described himself? "A poet who teaches as a public service"—was that what he'd said? Of course, he was in the bag, Balzic thought. Then again, *in vino veritas*. In boozo, trutho. . . .

He looked around the den, stepping over to the shelves of

books behind the walnut and stainless steel desk. He ran his fingers over the shelves and then over the tops of three or four books. The Beverleys had an efficient and dedicated cleaning woman.

He took note of the desk. Everything was in order, making Balzic wonder whether Beverley did any work here. The room seemed more a refuge than a shop. The few pencils in the leather-covered oval container had been recently sharpened, or perhaps they had been sharpened some time ago and never used.

Balzic lit a cigarette, not because he wanted to smoke, but because he wanted to throw a match and the ashes in the ashtray on the desk. He had just flicked off the first ash when the door opened and a short, compactly built man in his mid-thirties came in, closing the door quietly but firmly behind him. He stepped briskly toward Balzic with his hand extended, saying, "I'm Dr. Beverley. And you're?"

"Balzic. I'm chief of police here," he said, shaking hands and watching Beverley's eyes to see if he glanced at the ashtray.

Beverley didn't look at the ashtray but said, "There's an ashtray on the desk."

It amounted to the same thing, Balzic thought, suppressing a smile.

"Sorry to keep you waiting," Beverley said. "My wife neglected to tell me that you'd called earlier. I, uh, assume it's important."

"It is. One of your students is dead."

Beverley's face drained of color and for a second it appeared he was going to lose his balance. He recovered quickly and said, "I presume from the way you said that, uh, that it was not—that it was unnatural."

"You presume right. She was murdered—"

Beverley wavered and had to support himself on the desk. "Oh, good Lord."

"We don't know when exactly, but our first guess is that it happened at least a week ago. We won't know for sure until we get the coroner's report."

"My God, that's awful. Terrible."

"In more ways than one," Balzic said. "The semester's over, right?"

"Huh? Oh yes. The last exams were given today. Who was it?"

"Name was Janet Pisula. She lived with Miss Summer. Rented there, I mean. We've talked to all the people there except one and we'll get to him as soon as he gets off work, but we're going to need all the help we can get from you."

"Certainly. Of course. Anything I can do, just say it . . . my God, this is awful."

"Yeah, well, I get the drift of what you're thinking, Dr. Beverley, but it, uh, was a hell of a lot worse for her than it's going to be for you or the school."

Beverley flushed. "I'm sorry. I—"

Balzic held up his hand. "Say nothing. What I want to know right now is if there is any way you can notify the students here to stay around. They get away from us now, we're going to be chasing all over the county trying to run down whatever information they might have, and it would make things a lot simpler if you keep as many of them around as you could."

"I don't see how," Beverley said. "Most of them have left already. Some finished with their exams yesterday. There were a number who finished Wednesday. There would be no reason for them to remain here unless they were planning to attend the summer sessions. Even so, they would more than likely have left because the summer session, the first one, the six-week session, doesn't begin for three weeks."

"Well how about the ones who took exams today and tonight? Is there any way you could get word out to them to stay put?"

"That's going to be rather difficult."

"Uh, Dr. Beverley, there isn't any of this going to be easy, I'll tell you straight. We don't have diddly-damn to go on so far, and the people we've talked to already haven't given us a damn thing except that the girl kept pretty much to herself. We also know she wasn't robbed, and we've got pretty fair odds she wasn't raped, and that's about it. Which means, in short, that we've got a lot of talking to do to a hell of a lot of people. Which means, furthermore, that all the people you can keep close for a while is going to make it just a little bit easier. Not much, but a little. So if you can get the word out, I'd appreciate it."

"Yes, of course, I understand what you're saying, chief, but I don't even know where to begin. We don't have dormitories. All our students live wherever they can. A great number of them commute."

"Well you must have a list of students. Somebody has to have a roster with addresses, right?"

"Right. Of course."

"Well would you mind picking up that phone and calling whoever that might be and asking him to get over here with that roster?"

Beverley flushed again. "Certainly." He reached for the phone and then rubbed his temples. "What am I thinking about?" he said to himself more than to Balzic. "He's here now. In the living room."

"Oh sweet Jesus," Balzic said to himself, turning his back as Beverley wheeled about and went out. A minute later he returned with two men, both in their mid-to-late thirties, both dressed casually, and both looking as concerned as the amount they'd obviously had to drink would allow.

"Chief Balzic," Beverley said, "this is Roy Weintraub, our treasurer, and this is Dr. Larry Ellis, our academic dean."

K.C. CONSTANTINE

"Gentlemen," Balzic said, shaking hands.

"I haven't told them what this is about, chief," Beverley said. "I just told them that it was extremely important."

Balzic nodded. "I'll keep it brief, gentlemen. A student of yours, one Janet Pisula, was murdered approximately a week ago and—"

Weintraub's hand shot to his mouth. Ellis's lips parted and he sucked in a breath with an audible hiss.

"—as I was saying, so far we have practically nothing to go on. All the people we've talked to either didn't know the girl or, if they did, they hardly spoke to her. The only person who did speak with her often was her landlady, Miss Cynthia Summer, and if you know Miss Cynthia, you probably also know she had a stroke not too long ago, which means she can't remember very much about the girl except that she was kind and pretty lonely.

"I've already learned from Dr. Beverley," Balzic went on, "that most of the students have gone home for the summer and that a lot of others are commuters. What I want from you gentlemen is a roster of students—with addresses."

"Are you assuming it was another student?" Ellis asked.

"We're not assuming much of anything right now. What we want the roster for is to try and find somebody who knew this girl, knew something about her, knew who she was with, maybe knew somebody who wanted to be with her. And when I say I want a roster with addresses, naturally I mean both addresses. Home addresses and addresses of the places where they lived in town."

"Well, home addresses are easy to obtain," Weintraub said. "They'll be on permanent record cards. But residences here are another matter."

"Why's that?"

"Because we just don't have one. We don't keep track of who

44

rents rooms to students," Weintraub said. "Our experience has been that students move around a lot anyway. They're always looking for ways to save money—moving in and out with one another. And that's perfectly understandable."

"Then how do you go about finding a student in an emergency? What do you do—wait until they show up in class or what?"

Weintraub, Ellis, and Beverley looked sheepishly at one another.

Balzic cleared his throat and waited. When he got no response he said, "Well, gentlemen, I'm not about to start telling you how to run your college. That's out of my line. But right now, I've got a problem, and I'd like to hear some suggestions."

"About what?" Weintraub asked.

"Hey, goddammit," Balzic snapped, "maybe you didn't hear me right. One of your students is dead. Murdered. That was five, six, maybe eight days ago. We won't know for sure until we get the coroner's report tomorrow. In the meantime, whoever killed her is still walking around, and nobody gave us any guarantee he won't get it in his head to do it again. So you people better get organized. I want some names and addresses. Everybody connected with this college—faculty, students, custodial people—everybody. And I want them now. What do I have to do—drive you all over to Conemaugh General so you can watch the autopsy?"

"Uh, Chief Balzic," Beverley said, "if you'll give us a moment to discuss this, I'm sure we can provide you with what you need, and I give you my word, you'll have our full cooperation on this."

"All right," Balzic said, going to the door. "I need to use your bathroom anyway." He shut the door to the den and knocked on the door to the bathroom. When he heard nothing, he opened it.

Inside, the short blocky woman with the blue tee-shirt and the bullish man who had looked familiar to Balzic reluctantly broke apart from what had obviously been a strenuous kiss. Rather, the bullish man tried to break away. He dropped his arms and backed up, but the woman clung to him and only the sink against his backside prevented him from losing his balance entirely.

"Excuse me," Balzic said, looking away. "I didn't hear anybody say anything when I knocked."

"That's all right," the woman said. "We don't mind."

"Uh, I'm sure you don't, but I'd like to use the facility."

"The what?"

"The toilet. You know. You got one painted on your shirt."

"Oh well. You can't use this one. I mean, it's already in use."

"I can see that. But I really do have to use the one on the floor. The one behind you?"

"Be our guest," the woman said.

"You're not going to leave?"

"Leave? Whatever for?" she said. "I mean, my God, man, it's just a simple biological function. You don't have to have a doctorate or anything."

Balzic nodded several times, muttering, "Yeah," each time. "Well," he said, slipping past the woman and unzipping his fly, "when in Rome and all that . . . teachers, huh." He shook his head and caught a glimpse of the woman grinning at him.

"What's so funny?"

"Oh, I was just making a bet with myself. I bet you were the kind who got down on one knee so you wouldn't sound like a shower. I guess I lost."

"You made a study of that, huh?"

"I know Rocco does it that way, and you two look like you've got other things in common."

The bullish man groaned and rolled his eyes.

Balzic zipped his fly and pushed the toilet lever. "Rocco," he said, "your last name wouldn't be Cimoli, would it? The reason I'm asking is when I saw you two dancing out in the living room, I had the feeling I knew you from someplace. Am I right?"

"Yeah. Yeah, you're right," Rocco said, putting his thick hands on the sink to support himself as the woman continued to lean into him. He looked suddenly apprehensive.

"Uh, young lady," Balzic said, "if you don't mind, I'd—"

"I do mind. I am not a lady. I am a woman."

"Okay. Uh, woman, would you mind very much excusing us? I got something I want to talk to Rocco about."

"I most certainly do mind. I have things I want to *do* with Rocco, and I'm not about to go sit with the ladies while you boys talk about football."

"Have it your way, woman," Balzic said, facing Rocco. "Rocco, you correct me if I'm wrong, but the last time I saw you, you were crawling in the back of the sheriff's wagon on your way to Southern Regional. That was about, oh, four, maybe five years ago—am I right?"

"Six years ago," Rocco said, closing his eyes and pursing his lips.

"Rocco!" the woman nearly shouted. "You were in prison?"

He opened his eyes and nodded slowly.

"That's great!" she said, throwing her arms around his neck and trying to kiss him on the mouth, but missing because he turned his face away and began to pull her arms from around his neck.

"Come on, willya. I mean, Jesus . . ."

"Rocco, what's wrong? That's terrific that you were in prison. You never told me. Why didn't you tell me? Oh, we have lots of things to talk about now. And do. And doooo. Do we ever!"

Rocco took the woman by one arm and moved her toward the door. For a second she looked as though she was going to resist, but Rocco's strength surprised her. She even began to look a little frightened.

"Rocco, you're hurting me."

"That's right, I am. 'Cause I want you to leave and I don't want to hear anything about the National Organization for Women or anything like it. I have some things I got to say to the chief, and they're not about football. And one more thing," he said, pushing the door shut again after he'd started to open it, "you get out there in that living room, you just forget what you heard in here, you hear me? I mean, I know you like to tell the people what you think the people ought to know and all that jazz, but you just put a lock on your mouth, honey, 'cause if you don't, I *will* hurt you."

"Rocco . . ."

"Go, baby. Now." Rocco pushed her out the door, shut it, and locked it.

"Okay, Rocco, let's have it."

"Okay. Straight. And I know you'll check the papers."

Balzic nodded. "I will."

"I got eleven and a half to twenty-three. I did thirteen months and out. I finished high school in there, and when I got out I went to West Chester State. I got a bachelor of science in physical education, and I did it in three years. I worked my ass off. I pumped gas, washed dishes, swept locker rooms, worked in a laundry. I never cheated on a test, and I came out of there with better than a B average. And believe it or not, twelve more credit hours and I get my master's degree. And what you just saw is the first time I put my hands on anybody outside of a gym since you know when—for any reason. I even got into karate to learn how to control myself, and if I keep going the way I'm going, I'm going to have a black belt in about two years. In other words, man, I'm straight. I'm so straight that broad was right. I do go down on one knee so I won't make noise when I piss."

Balzic nodded. "Who knows?"

"One person too goddamn many right now."

"Rocco, you kidding yourself, or what? That even made the Pittsburgh papers."

"Hey, man. That was six years ago. Do you know there's not one person from this town on this faculty? They're all from out of town. Hell, most of them aren't even from Pennsylvania. And this place has only been in operation for three years."

"What about students? There have to be a lot of them who remember, right?"

"Well, all I can tell you is they never let on if they know. In fact, sometimes I get the impression the ones who do know, sort of, I don't know, look up to me, like I'm some sort of a guy who got trapped into something and then got himself untrapped—on his own. I don't know. Maybe that's just what I like to think." Rocco paused. "What about you? What are you going to do?"

"Me? I'm not going to do a damn thing. Why should I? Be happy for you. Ask how your mother is, that's all."

"She's okay. I'm making enough now so that she doesn't have to do that shit anymore."

"You see her often?"

"Once a week, maybe twice. I make sure she's all right."

"Well, next time you see her, tell her I said hello."

"I'll do that," Rocco said, sighing and looking at his shoes.

"Let's forget about it, okay? Tell me about something else. You ever hear of a student here named Janet Pisula?"

"I don't know anything about the female students. You should ask Toni."

"She the one just in here?"

"Yeah. She's the girls' phys-ed teacher. She talks a lot of garbage, but she's all right. At least I hope she's all right. I don't know whether I wanted her to hear that."

"You think it would do some good for me to talk to her?"

"I doubt it. As far as she's concerned, you're an oink-oink. I'm surprised she let you off as easy as she did. Man, she can really put some bad mouth on people. Wow. Course, you broke her up when you blew her that kiss. I never saw her laugh that hard at anything any man ever did. I mean, except when she's laughing at them. But when she was laughing at you, that was real. She really enjoyed that."

There was a knock, and then Dr. Beverley's voice asked for Balzic. "Are you in there?"

"Maybe I'll talk to you later, Rocco," Balzic said, opening the door and confronting Beverley.

"I think we can get you what you want," Beverley said.

Balzic nodded and followed Beverley back into the den. He found Ellis and Weintraub staring blankly at one another, caught in that limbo between where the alcohol they'd drunk was starting to wear off and the reality of the situation was beginning to crowd in.

"You can get the rosters?" Balzic asked.

Ellis nodded. "Yes, but I wonder if it would be possible for someone to drive me to my office. I'm afraid I've had more than my share of party."

"No problem," Balzic said, going to the phone. He called his station and asked Stramsky to send a mobile unit. After he hung up, he told Ellis to take the rosters to the Summer house and turn them over to Johnson.

50

Ellis nodded and said, "I think I better have some coffee while I'm waiting."

"Wouldn't be a bad idea," Balzic said. Turning to Beverley, he asked, "How many people from your English department are here?"

"All of them, I think."

"How about getting them in here, will you please?"

Beverley followed Ellis and Weintraub to the door, but stopped. "You mean one at a time or—"

"No, no. All of them."

Beverley left and returned a minute later leading Malcolm Keenan and three other men. All had had too much party and were trying, with the exception of Keenan, to look properly somber. Beverley excused himself without making introductions, saying that he had to explain to his wife what was going on, and Keenan took command, or tried to, at once. He made the introductions, mispronouncing Balzic's name each time as he presented Joseph Winoski, James Farrell, and Edward Snavely.

Snavely gave the appearance of a man who worked at trying to disgust others. He had one button missing from his shirt, another missing from the front of his suit coat, and still another missing from his sleeve. He seemed unable or unwilling to open his mouth fully when speaking so that saliva bubbled at the corners of his mouth, and he kept inhaling the mucus in his nose with a sound that must have set his students' skin crawling. He weighed easily two hundred seventy pounds and was adding to his girth with a beer and a salami and cheese sandwich plastered with yellow mustard. When he shook Balzic's hand, mustard dripped on the rug. A man, Balzic thought, who did everything he could to make certain no one got close to him, probably bemoaning the fact all the while.

Joseph Winoski was as neat as Snavely was sloppy: his

ankle-high boots seemed spit-polished, his double-knit suit, though a conservative blue-gray check, was up to the minute in cut, and his build was of a man who spent his lunch hours in the YMCA gym. Balzic could smell Winoski's after-shave lotion as they shook hands, a brand advertised on television by seamen and adventurers, and could feel the hours at the gym in the handshake. He couldn't help wondering how Winoski would react if he were told that he was just a step away from Snavely in motive, that his neatness probably had the same fear behind it as Snavely's sloppiness. Somebody who told Winoski that would more than likely have to learn what sort of physical shape he was in, Balzic thought, resisting his urge to smile.

James Farrell was the only one of the four who seemed at ease with himself. He dressed, moved, and spoke like a thousand other men who would have been lost in crowds. His only distinction seemed to be that he had no distinction, except for his name, which, when Balzic said the name sounded familiar, he said was the result of his father's love of author James T. Farrell. "He used to call me Studs when I was a kid."

"I don't get the connection," Balzic said.

"My namesake wrote a book, well, three books actually, called *Studs Lonigan,* and my father loved them so much, he took it out on me." He smiled when he said it, without the slightest trace of resentment.

"You never heard of *Studs Lonigan?*" Snavely asked, his mouth full of sandwich.

"Sorry," Balzic said. "I just thought the name sounded familiar."

"Well, chief," Keenan said, "don't you think you ought to tell us what this is about?"

"Sure. But first I'd like you to get my name straight. It's not Ballsy. It's Balzic."

"Sorry about that," Keenan said, laughing much too hard and then putting his hand on Balzic's shoulder and saying, "No offense intended—or no intense offended, whichever the case may be."

Balzic nodded. "Yeah, sure. Okay, gentlemen, here's the problem. One of your students was murdered. Her name was Janet Pisula." He watched their faces as he spoke. Their reaction seemed genuine enough: Snavely and Winoski looked astonished at first and then baffled; Keenan and Farrell looked plainly shocked.

"Did you say Janet Pisula?" Keenan asked.

"Yes. And I understand she was in your composition class last semester. What I want to know, among other things, is whose class she was in this semester?"

"She was in my section," Farrell said, shaking his head. "Little Miss Nobody."

"All right," Balzic said. "Mr. Snavely, Mr. Winoski, unless you know something about this girl, you can leave."

"I never heard of her," Winoski said.

"Neither did I," Snavely said, chewing his sandwich as though he had forgotten how to swallow.

"You know nothing about her—never heard anything about her?"

Snavely and Winoski both shrugged and shook their heads, waiting a moment longer until Balzic nodded toward the door, and then left.

"All right, Mr. Keenan, Mr. Farrell, whatever you know."

"I think I should begin," Keenan said, "but since, uh, I mean, I had no idea—I think I better get some coffee. I've really had a lot—no more than my usual, understand, but . . ."

"Go ahead," Balzic said. "Why don't you see if you can bring back the pot? If it won't be too much trouble for the host."

"Of course. I'll do that," Keenan said, leaving the room.

"Mr. Farrell," Balzic said, "a minute ago when you said the girl was in your section, I think I heard you say something about little Miss Nobody,' am I right?"

Farrell nodded. "Yes, I did. That's the way she struck me."

"How did she strike you? What did she do? What didn't she do?"

"That's just it. She didn't do much of anything. I can't recall ever hearing her say anything at all in class. She just sat there, looking pretty much bewildered. Sometimes when I'd call on her, ask her opinion about something we were discussing, she wouldn't answer. She'd start to say something, and then she'd— she'd just go mute. Literally dumb. As though some circuitry between her brain and her voice box had been shorted. She looked as though she would have given anything to be able to say something, not necessarily something intelligent or brilliant or even charming—but she apparently couldn't say anything."

"Did you ever talk to her privately about it?"

"Yes, I tried to. Twice, as a matter of fact. Privately, it was even worse. She was petrified. She couldn't speak at all. All she could do was nod her head and blush. I never had a student like her before—of course, this is only my third year of teaching. The second time, I tried to suggest to her that she might do well to get some kind of counseling. I must've approached it completely wrong because she practically ran out of my office. It was embarrassing."

"Embarrassing?"

"Well, the fact is, I like to think of myself as knowing something about communication. After all, that is supposed to be my profession, and there she was, a person with whom I couldn't communicate at all. She brought me face to face with my limits. That's what I meant by embarrassing."

"How did you suggest it to her, about getting counseling?"

"I don't recall what I said exactly. I think I told her that she had to have some kind of blockage, that it didn't seem logical or even sensible that she should be able to write the way she did and then on the other hand, have so much trouble talking."

"Was she a very good writer?"

"Oh yes. One of the best. She had a very good eye for detail. Her papers were always filled with solid examples of the abstractions she used. That's something you generally have trouble with in freshman comp. Freshmen are generally in love with abstractions. I keep trying to tell them that the further removed one is from fact the more difficult it is for one person to understand another."

"I take your meaning," Balzic said, "but that's damn strange. Because I'll tell you, the one person who seemed to know anything about her—I mean the one person I've talked to so far—another student, a girl named Patricia Keim—do you know her?"

Farrell shook his head.

"Well, the Keim girl said just the opposite of what you said. She said that was the one thing the Pisula girl couldn't do. She said one of their assignments the first semester was to take an abstraction and break it down, and the Keim girl said she tried to explain to the Pisula girl how to go about it. I think she said she told her to take a season of the year and write everything solid she could think of when she thought of that season. But the Keim girl said that the Pisula girl wasn't even aware that a season of the year was an abstraction. Now how do you figure that?"

Farrell shrugged. "I can't figure it. I don't understand it at all. Unless..."

"Unless what?"

"Well, unless she took a great jump in understanding. Sometimes a student may not be able to comprehend what you're saying for a long time, and then suddenly, for no reason that anyone can explain, the insight comes to them. It's not uncommon; In fact, it's the thing you hope for, the thing you hope will happen in a classroom, or at least that's what I hope for. That's what bothered me so much about her. She wrote so well, yet she wasn't able to talk. Usually, it's just the reverse. They all talk well enough to be understood, given, of course, that they know what they're talking about, but when they sit down in front of that blank page, they just come unhinged."

"What did you say?"

"I said they come unhinged. Lose their confidence—"

"No, no. Before that. You said something about a blank page."

"Yeah. I said that some people talk well enough, but when they sit down in front of that blank page, they—"

"That's it."

"What's it?" Farrell said.

"Blank page."

"I don't understand. What's that have to do with this?"

Before Balzic could answer, though he was not saved from answering as much as he was saved from making up some reason for being concerned about a specific blank page, he saw the door being pushed open. Keenan came in with a large silver tray, balancing a pot of coffee, some mugs, and a creamer and sugar bowl.

Keenan poured, acting a perfect host, giving Balzic the impression that much of what Keenan did was an act. Balzic couldn't put his finger on why exactly, except that Keenan's smile and gestures while pouring were laced with an exuberance that seemed contrived, an exuberance Keenan immediately turned off the moment Balzic asked him what he knew about Janet Pisula. Then Keenan switched faces at once, going from perfect host to concerned head of department, from smiling waiter to frowning, fretful witness to tragedy.

"I can't tell you very much about her at all," Keenan said. "I can only, in all candor, give you some impressions. I found her to be as inarticulate as any student I've ever had—and I don't mean to say for a moment that I had her."

Balzic had to turn his back to Keenan to keep from telling him to shut off the nonsense.

"That was not meant as a pun, I assure you," Keenan said quickly when Balzic turned back to him. "I wanted that to be clear. The reason I want that clear is that, well, I have somewhat of a reputation as a, well, uh, a seeker of pleasure."

"You fuck around with your students," Balzic said evenly.

"Yes. You could put it that way. Well, not exactly that way—"

"And you don't want me to get the idea that there might be some connection between you and Janet Pisula in that way."

"Yes. Right. Absolutely. Because there wasn't. She was, in a word, incommunicado. And I cannot make it with females who are incommunicado."

"Well, Mr. Keenan, now that we've eliminated that possibility, would you mind giving me some impressions that I could use?"

"Of course. Though I don't know what you mean when you say you need impressions you can use."

"Oh Jesus Christ, man, tell me what you know about her."

Keenan flushed. "Yes. Uh, well, as I said, she was incommunicado."

"Which means exactly what?"

"Which means she wouldn't respond verbally. Anywhere. In class or out."

"I see. What was your reaction to her?"

"Well, to be perfectly candid, I thought she was rather doltish. Not someone on whom I should waste my energy. She was one of the thousands too many young people who don't belong in any college classroom taking up the space. In my opinion she would have been much better off touring the country on a bicycle or waiting tables at some resort near the ocean."

"Uh-huh," Balzic said, "and what did you think of her writing?"

"Incredibly bad. Worse. Atrocious." Keenan reflected for a moment. "Except for near the end of the semester. Then, as I recall, she turned in a couple of papers that were very good. So good, in fact, they made me suspicious. And then when she took the final, I was sure of my suspicions. I had to get drunk to give her a D."

Farrell, who had been listening calmly, suddenly couldn't keep his hands still. "You had to do what?"

"Get flat out stoned," Keenan said. "Sober, I couldn't have given her a Z."

"I don't believe that," Farrell said. "She was one of the best writers in my section."

Keenan shook his head. "Jim, just as a friend and absolutely not as department chairman, I'd have to say she may have *known* the best writer in your section, but there's no way she could have *been* the best writer in anybody's section. I'm making no judgments about her as a person, you understand, but, well, no one with her limited ability should be in college. I'm sorry."

"I can't believe you said that," Farrell said, jamming his hands into his pockets and hunching his shoulders.

"Well," Keenan said, "there it is."

"Uh, let's get off this," Balzic said. "Let's get on to something solid. Mr. Keenan, who was she with, who did you see her with, who did you see trying to be with her?"

"Nobody. I can't recall ever seeing her with anybody. I don't recall ever seeing her talking to anyone. She'd come into class, sit in the seat nearest the door, keep her head buried in her notebook most of the class, and she'd leave as soon as I dismissed the class."

"Mr. Farrell, how about you?"

"She did exactly the same thing in my class. Even to the point of sitting in the seat closest to the door."

"You never saw her talking to anyone?"

Farrell shook his head. "And I've already told you about the times I tried to talk to her out of class."

"Hmm," Balzic said. "Anything else? Anything at all?"

"Nothing," Keenan said. Farrell just shook his head and jammed his hands deeper into his pockets.

"Then I guess that's all, gentlemen," Balzic said. "Just do me a favor. When you go back out there, tell anybody who had her in class to come in here, will you?"

"Certainly," Keenan said. 'Would you, uh, like more coffee, or would you like me to take the tray out?"

"Suit yourself. I don't want any more coffee. You can take the tray." Balzic watched them go, fuming to himself about what he'd just heard. It made no sense. A girl who never talked to anyone. That was impossible. There had to be someone. Someone who knew her well enough to know she lived alone, someone who knew her well enough to know she probably wouldn't make a sound if she got in trouble. Then again, whoever killed her didn't have to know any such thing. Whoever killed her didn't have to know a damned thing about her—except that he wanted her dead.

* * *

Moments after Keenan and Farrell left, Balzic went to the phone and dialed the Summer house.

"Summer residence, Lieutenant Johnson speaking."

"Walk? Mario. My man get there with the dean?"

"About two minutes ago. He's still here."

"Well, I busted into a party at the president's house. Most of the faculty is here. There might be a couple missing, I don't know. But right now, from the ones I've talked to so far, I'm getting nothing. The only thing anybody's agreed on is that the girl wasn't one for talking. What d'you come up with?"

"About the same," Johnson said. "Our print man won't know for sure until tomorrow, but as of right now, his best guess is that all the prints in the room belonged to the girl. Except for a couple on the door which probably belong to you."

"Yeah. Did you talk to those two across the hall again?"

"Yep. They say the same things. Didn't hear anything, didn't see anything—except for that guy one of them thinks he saw, but he still can't say anything definite about that guy. Now he thinks the guy was young and white, but he shakes his head everytime I ask him if he thinks he could identify the guy. And they swear they weren't out of their room except to go to class, take tests, and eat."

"How about the Cerovich kid—he come back from work yet?"

"Yeah. He's a zero, too. He never even saw her. Her name didn't mean a thing. And we know where he's been every night for the last year. Course, what we don't know is time of death. So he's still a remote possibility. But from talking to him, I'd say no. He's too goddamn solid. He wasn't here five minutes and he had two phone calls from broads. Good-looking kid. Probably getting more ass than a toilet seat. Guys like that just don't kill broads. You didn't get anything at all from her teachers?"

"I haven't talked to all of them yet. I just talked to her

composition teachers so far. One of them thinks she was the best writer in his section. The other one, the chairman of the department, thinks she was the worst. He suspected her of cheating, still thinks she was, and told the other one, the one who thinks she was the best—he told him he'd been suckered. But both of them agree, the girl talked not at all. Big fucking deal."

"Yeah."

"Hey. Did her guardians, her aunt and uncle, did they show yet?"

"No, but I got a confirmation they were notified, so they should be pulling in soon. If they don't need a doctor."

"Oh boy. Well, I'm going to hang in here a while. There are a couple more teachers I want to talk to. You going to stay there?"

"I'll have to until the relatives show. Christ, that's going to be fun. How 'bout you taking them up to identify the body?"

"Up yours, buddy. That's one party I don't need." Balzic was going to hang up, but then said quickly, "Hey, Walk, when the dean showed with the rosters, did he have one for local addresses for the students?"

"No. He apologized all over the place for that. But what could I say? He didn't have it, he didn't have it."

"If that isn't bad enough, when I asked the president if there was any way he could keep the students here, he just shook his head. That's when I found out they didn't have local addresses. Christ almighty . . ."

"How much longer you think you'll be there?"

Balzic looked over his shoulder as the door opened and a man and a woman walked in. "Not long," he said to Johnson. "I think the last of her teachers are coming in right now. Soon as I finish with them I'll be down." He hung up and introduced himself to the two who had come in.

The woman, short, roundish, in her late thirties, with no

makeup and her hair cut severely short, introduced herself as Miss Ulishney. "Janet was in my advanced shorthand course," she said somberly.

The man, shorter than the woman, a collar of jet black hair flowing downward around his ears but shiny bald on top, shook Balzic's hand and introduced himself as Phil Castro. "The girl was in my American history course, but I'll tell you right now and save us both a lot of time. I know practically nothing about her except that she never missed class and that she was just an average student. A low C student, and her grades were more a matter of my generosity than her effort."

"Mr. Castro, did you ever see her talking to anybody? Ever see anybody talking to her?"

"I never paid attention to that sort of thing."

"Uh-huh. Where did she sit in your class?"

"Sit? What does that have to do with anything?"

"Just tell me, if you can remember."

"I remember that clearly. Last seat, last row. Right next to the door."

Balzic nodded. "Well, unless you can tell me something more than that, you can go."

"All I can tell you is that the last time I saw her was last Wednesday, the next to the last class, and the only class she missed was the last class."

"That next to last class, that would've been, uh, the twenty-sixth of May, right?"

"That's right. Last class was the twenty-eighth of May. Last Friday."

"Well, thanks for your help. But if you think of anything, call me at City Hall or call Lieutenant Johnson at Troop A, Rocksburg Barracks."

"I'm sorry I can't be of more help," Castro said. "I'm sorry that it happened. How did it happen, by the way? Nobody out there seems to know."

"Let's just say she was murdered and let it go at that, okay?"

Castro shrugged and left.

"Miss Ulishney, I hope you can tell me more than that."

"I wish I could," she said. "I just feel very bad for her. But I really don't know much about her."

"She was quiet, she didn't talk to anybody, she didn't say much in class—are those your impressions of her? I'm asking, not to put words in your mouth, but because those are the impressions everyone else seems to have."

"I'm afraid I have to go along with the rest. I really can't recall saying anything to the girl."

"Your class was probably all girls, right?"

"Yes. All my classes are. I also teach business math and office machines."

"How was she in your class, as a student, I mean."

"Not very good, I'm afraid. Oh, she mastered the short-hand characters well enough, but she wasn't nearly as fast as she should have been. I think her top speed was no more than eighty-five words a minute. Not nearly fast enough for an advanced class. She should have been able to take at least a hundred words a minute."

"Good but slow."

"Well, not really good either, because when I played my practice tapes at a hundred words a minute, she would natu-rally miss a lot. She was really competent only when I played the slower tapes."

"I see. Uh, one more thing. Well, two more. When did you see her last, one, and two, where did she sit in your class?"

"I saw her last Wednesday. Yes, I'm sure of that because I remember that she didn't come to last Friday's class and I remembered thinking how unusual that was. She hadn't missed a class for two semesters."

"And where did she sit?"

"Like Phil—Mr. Castro, I mean—I don't understand that question, but I'll answer it. She sat in the middle of the front row. Right in front of my desk. Why do you ask that?"

"I'm not sure. It's just that her two English teachers, Keenan and Farrell, happened to mention it as though it was important, and then when I asked Mr. Castro—well, you heard what he said. Seems the only thing you people are sure of about this girl was where she sat. That, plus she wasn't a very good student, plus the other thing everybody's agreed on, which is, she didn't say anything, or as little as she could and still get by." Balzic scratched his chin. "Is there anybody else out there who had her in class? So far, I count three courses she was taking. Yours, Mr. Castro's, and Mr. Farrell's. Would that be a full schedule?"

"No. A full schedule is generally twelve to fourteen hours, but I doubt that half our students take a full schedule. Most can't afford it. A great many of them work part-time, and most are from lower-middle-income families."

Balzic thanked her for her help and then went to the door and opened it for her. "Just one more thing, Miss Ulishney. Take a quick survey for me out there, will you please? Ask if there's anybody else who knew her."

"Certainly," she said, going past him.

Balzic left the door open and stood rocking on his heels and toes. It was only then that he noticed he'd stopped perspiring and that he knew the reason: J. Hale Beverley's house was more than adequately air-conditioned. He was thinking about the broken fan back in his office when the blocky woman, the one Rocco Cimoli called Toni, came striding through the doorway and had to stop short to keep from bumping into him.

He backed up and pursed his lips. Apparently she'd responded affirmatively to Miss Ulishney's survey, but Balzic wasn't sure he wanted to ask this Toni, whatever her information, much of anything. He had the feeling that whatever she was going to say about Janet Pisula was going to be starched with feminist propaganda.

"Uh, we didn't meet before, in the bathroom, I mean. Rocco told me your first name was Toni. Your last name?"

"Rosario."

"Uh, Miss Rosario—"

"Pronounce that miz, if you don't mind."

Balzic shook his head and started to laugh.

"What's so funny?"

"Oh, I was just wondering what you say to guys with speech problems. You know, the guys who talk like thith? Or hasn't that Come up in your meetings yet?"

For the briefest moment, Toni Rosario looked almost ready to laugh at herself, but she instantly put her fences back up and said, "Well, so we haven't got around to that, but I'll tell you what. If that girl had listened to me, she might've grown up to be a woman."

"She was a student of yours then. In your gym class?"

"She was. And I told her just like I told all the others, just like I *tried* to tell all the others, that they would have to learn how to protect themselves."

"The beasties are all around, right?"

"That's right, they are."

"And if she'd just listened to you and learned karate or judo or something, she'd still be alive today, right?"

"Exactly right. No man would've been able to rape her, never mind kill her."

"Well, Miz Rosario, I hate to spoil all your fun, but as far as we know—though we won't know for sure until we hear from the coroner—but right now we're pretty sure she wasn't raped, and, uh, there's nothing really to tell us that it was a man who killed her."

"Well out there," she said, pointing testily in the direction of the living room, "everybody's saying she was raped."

"I have no idea what they're saying out there. A couple minutes ago a guy walked in, Castro his name was, and he gave me the impression nobody knew what happened. Now you come in saying everybody's got the information."

"Well? How did it happen?"

"All I'm going to tell you is what I told the others. The girl was murdered, and she's been dead at least a week, maybe longer. And whoever did it did it very quietly 'cause she didn't make a sound—or else everybody where she lived is deaf."

"Well, that sounds like her, not making a peep. A regular house-mouse. She couldn't do this, she couldn't do that—"

"You mean in gym class?"

"Well of course. Where else would I come in contact with her?"

"I don't know. You tell me."

"Well I didn't. She was in my gym class for two semesters and half the time she'd just stand around looking like something out of a Victorian novel. Like if somebody touched her, she'd just crumble into a heap of sugar and spice and everything nice. Gawd."

"What did she say about standing around? I mean, what reason did she give? Did she have a doctor's excuse for not doing anything?"

"Well, if she'd had a doctor's excuse, she wouldn't have even been there. There wasn't anything wrong with her. Nothing but a stupid, simpering idea that a woman was supposed to be delicate and fragile and weak."

"Did she say that or is that your conclusion?"

"It's my conclusion."

"Ever think you might've been wrong?"

"I'm not wrong about her. One day, gawd, I had them playing field hockey and one of the girls got a bloody nose. It was an accident. She got hit in the nose with the ball and it bled a little. It was nothing. I got it stopped in about two seconds, but the next thing I knew somebody was tapping me on the shoulder and telling me we had other problems. And there she was. Janet Pisula. Stretched out on the ground. Fainted. It was disgusting."

"Didn't you ask her about it? Didn't you check around about her? I mean, there might have been some reason why she was like that. I don't know what happened to her parents, but I do know she doesn't have any. She was raised by an aunt and uncle."

"So? Lots of people don't have parents. That's why there are orphanages."

"So you're telling me that because a lot of people are able to accept being orphans, uh, everybody should, is that it?"

"Everybody has things happen to them. You adapt. What's the big production?"

"And those people who can't adapt?"

"Oh bullshit," she said.

Balzic chewed the inside of his cheek. "Well, let's get back to Janet Pisula."

"I thought that's who we were talking about."

"More or less. But mostly what you've told me is what you thought of her. You haven't really told me what you know about her."

"Well then, I guess I don't know anything about her."

"Boy, I'll tell you something. I never met a bunch of people who know as little about a person as you people do. The girl was one of your students. Do you all know that little about all your students?"

"Do you have any idea how many students I come in contact with each semester?"

"Don't give me that, Miz Rosario. Do you know how many people there are in this town?"

"Are you going to tell me you know them all? Gawd."

"No. But I know the ones in trouble, and if I don't know them myself, then I go find somebody who does."

"Still—"

"Still nothing," Balzic said. "There are a lot more people with some kind of trouble in this town than there are students in this college—ah, forget it. That's all. You can go—oh, one more thing." Balzic stepped around her and closed the door. "What you heard in the bathroom, you didn't hear."

"About Rocco?"

"That's right. Do him and yourself a big favor, and forget you heard it. And don't get your head full of those goofy ideas I see wheeling around in your eyes. Because I'm going to tell you what he did—for one reason and one reason only. I don't like people walking around with bad information. And I'm really going out on a limb telling you this. You better not make me think I made a mistake."

She shifted her weight to one foot and crossed her arms. "It can't be all that bad."

"With some of the ideas you have, it could be dynamite."

"I'm not a complete ass."

"I hope not. Because what he did was kill a guy. He beat him to death with a baseball bat. And he did it because the guy called his mother a whore. The thing was, she was a whore, and Rocco knew it, and the reason he knew it was because she told him she was.

"I didn't know the family at that time," Balzic went on, "and the only reason I found out about it was because she'd gone to a priest and asked him whether she should tell Rocco or not. This was a couple years before this thing happened, and the priest advised her to tell him. I didn't agree with the priest's reasons for telling her to tell him, but it was over by the time I found out about it. I didn't find out until the priest came to me, which was after Rocco killed the guy.

"I was out of town when it happened. Rocco went into a bar to pick up a pizza, and while he was waiting for it, he overheard two guys talking, and one of them was really putting his mother down for doing what she was doing. He took the pizza home and went back with the bat. The owner of the bar was a friend of mine and he knew I was out of town, so he called the state police. I didn't have a chance to do anything about it until right before the trial when the priest came to me and gave me the background. I'm not trying to make myself out a big man, but if it wasn't for me going to the judge Rocco would've got life. He would've done thirteen years instead of thirteen months. And tonight's the second time in my life I've seen him. The other time was when I said, when I saw him crawling in the back of the sheriff's wagon."

"Oh wow."

"Oh wow is right, sister. Rocco's mother is still alive, and she loves her son more than she loves life itself. When she heard from the priest that I'd talked to the judge, she came to me, and if you think a minute, you'll know what she wanted to give me."

Toni canted her head. "Oh, now wait. Are you going to try and tell me that you didn't take it?"

"No. I took it," Balzic said. "Because if I hadn't, I would've shamed her. Also," Balzic said, breaking into a wide smile, "she was a fine-looking woman."

"If that isn't the most typical male bullshit I ever heard—"

"Listen. You think what you want, but that—what I just told you about Rocco's mother and me—that is exactly why you aren't going to say anything to him or about him. 'Cause like I said, I don't like people going around with bad information, and I just gave you good information. All there is. So take it in and then forget it." Balzic studied her face. "Think about it this way. Rocco didn't kill that guy because his mother was a whore. He knew that. He killed the guy because the guy put her down for being what she was. And I did what I did for him and I took what I took from her because that's the way it should have been. I told you because I didn't want you saying, in a party or someplace, something stupid like, 'Tell us what prison was like, Rocco,' or 'Hey, everybody, you want to hear from a real victim of a sexist society?'"

"And what would happen if I did?"

"You just might get to be questioned about who did what to your face, if you know what I mean. Rocco's not the kind of guy you fool around with. Now, unless there's something, else you can tell me about Janet Pisula?"

She shook her head and then stood a moment, shifting her weight from one foot to the other, looking confused, then aggressive, then regretful. She started to say something, but then shook her head and stepped past Balzic and opened the door and went out, leaving Balzic hoping weakly that he had not made a mistake in telling her. He knew he had to hope that he'd done right, otherwise he had left himself wide open for a problem. What he'd said about Rocco Cimoli not being the kind of guy you fool with was as true for him as it was for Toni Rosario. "Be right, you big man," he said to himself as he left the den and went into the kitchen.

He found Dr. and Mrs. Beverley facing each other but both staring at the floor, sharing a tense silence.

"Uh, Dr. Beverley," he said, "I think I've learned all I can here. For now anyway. If anybody thinks of anything, tell them to call me down at City Hall or Lieutenant Walker Johnson at Troop A Barracks, okay?"

"Yes. Of course." Beverley moved as though to show Balzic out.

"Don't bother," Balzic said. "I can find my way. Goodnight, and, uh, I'm sorry I had to spoil your party."

Mrs. Beverley did not look up, and Dr. Beverley said nothing, leaning backward to put his rump against the sink. He'd moved farther away from it than he'd thought and hit it with a thump that caused him to throw out his hands to catch his balance, looking as though much more than his balance was at stake.

Johnson was leaning on a pillar on the portico with his thumbs hooked in his pockets when Balzic drove up to the Summer house.

"Whatta you know, Walk?"

"I know it's hot."

"You ought to try walking out of an air-conditioned house into this."

"I'd like to try walking into one."

"All your people gone?"

"There's one guy up there putting a lock on the door. I sent all the rest back with all the girl's notebooks, letters, anything she'd written in. I got three men going through that. Shouldn't take them too long. There wasn't too much."

"Grimes call?"

"Oh yeah. Small surprise there. Not only was she not raped, her hymen was still intact. A very inactive virgin." Johnson stretched and yawned. "You know, I didn't think a girl could get through eighteen years and still have one. You'd think she'd have broken it doing something. Riding a bike, running around in a gym class, something."

"Well, from what her gym teacher told me, she wasn't much for running around."

"What else did you get up there?"

"Not a hell of a lot. I told you most of it when I called you."

"You didn't get any more than that?"

"Just a couple of goofy little things. One—which isn't all that goofy—she passed out when another girl in her gym class got a bloody nose. Two, she was taking four courses: English, history, shorthand, and gym. Except for English, she had the same teachers this semester as she did last, so that makes three men and two women. Never mind the gym class, in the other classes where the men taught, she always sat in the seat next to the door. In the shorthand class with the woman, she sat right up front. First row, right in front of the teacher's desk. Three, the English teacher she had this semester, guy named Farrell, said something about certain people just coming unhinged when they sit down in front of a blank page. I looked at the guy real good when he said it, but it looked to me like something he was just used to saying."

"What was he talking about?"

"He was talking about how some people can talk pretty good, but when they have to write they just can't do it. From the way he said it, I gathered it's a pretty common thing. And Christ knows, whenever I have to write something I go through a shit fit—"

"Yeah. Me too."

"—it was just that he happened to use those words. 'Blank page,' or 'Blank paper'—no, it was page, and they jumped at me."

"Was he talking about her specifically?"

"Yes and no. Yes, if you believe the other teacher she had,

this Keenan guy, the department chairman, 'cause he thought the girl couldn't write worth a damn. I told you that on the phone."

Johnson nodded.

"And no, if you believe this Farrell, 'cause he thought the girl was the best writer in his class. Those two had a real difference of opinion over that. I mean, if I hadn't been there, I got the feeling those two would've had a pretty fair go-round over it. But that Keenan—what a ballbuster he is. He lets me in and he introduces himself, you know, with the handshake that dislocates your shoulder, and he says, 'Malcolm Keenan here. I'm a poet who teaches as a public service.' Then he started telling me these raunchy limericks, oh boy . . ."

"What do you make of her sitting close to the door with the men teachers—scared of men?"

"That's what it sounds like to me, but all I know is, that was the one thing all those men were certain of. Hey, you hear anything from her aunt and uncle?"

"Yeah. The woman collapsed. Had to get her to a hospital. And the uncle was shaking too bad to drive, so he's coming down in one of our units. He didn't want to come at all. Which is normal enough."

"How long ago you hear that?"

"Twenty minutes. Should be here in fifteen, twenty minutes."

"You got the rosters, right?"

"Hey, pal. You know how many people there are connected with this college? Close to seven hundred, that's all. Six hundred and twenty-one students. A hundred and four of them full-time. The rest taking two or one course. Then there's the faculty, the deans, assorted other bureaucrats, buildings and grounds people, janitors, charwomen, manager of the student union—oh, shit, from all over the county."

"Well, we start with the ones from in her classes. That cuts it down. That should get us under a hundred."

Johnson yawned again. "You know, Mario, we're starting close to home, but what do we do if it's a goddamn transient?"

"The first thing we do, Walk, is we don't even think like that."

"I always like to think the worst. Just to make myself comfortable. Like those two little girls, remember? In that town just north of Edinboro?"

"I remember reading about it."

"Yeah. Well, you know how many people we talked to with that? Over five hundred. More than a hundred grade school kids. And you know what we come up with? Nothing . . . that's what bothers me about this one. Those two little girls were strangled with their own clothes." Johnson stared off into the night. "Sure wish the hell it would rain."

The front door opened and a state trooper came out carrying a small tool chest. "Here's the keys, lieutenant," he said, handing Johnson two padlock keys.

Johnson thanked him and told him he could leave.

"So now we wait for the uncle," Johnson said, stepping off the porch and walking slowly toward his cruiser. "You coming?" he called over his shoulder.

"Yeah. I'll see you up at the barracks."

Michael Pisula came into Troop A's duty room on the arm of the state trooper who'd driven him. He was a short man, slender, with a slight paunch below his belt. His white shirt was sweat-stained and his trousers rumpled. He had a hanky wadded in his right hand and kept putting it to his mouth as he was directed to a chair. His eyes were raw and he had difficulty clearing his throat.

Balzic brought him a paper cup of water, but Pisula waved

it away. Then he broke down, weeping uncontrollably for what seemed to Balzic an hour, though it was not more than a minute.

"Who would do this to her?" he said after he'd got control. He had not asked Balzic or Johnson; he seemed to be asking as though praying.

"Mr. Pisula," Johnson said, "I know how difficult this is—"

"Difficult! My God, man, you don't have any idea what this girl's been through in her life. And then to, to—like this . . ."

Johnson and Balzic looked at each other, loathing to begin to ask the questions they knew had to be asked.

"Do you know," Pisula said suddenly, "she was just eighteen two weeks ago? The Sunday before last. She came home and we had a party for her. Ann made a beautiful cake. We had turkey. It was like Christmas. We were so happy for her she was finally getting out, getting to meet people. And she said she was doing so well and having such a good time. She kept saying how much she liked the people in her rooming house, how nice they were to her . . . now, my God—is there a God? Tell me. I'd like to know if there's a God. Would he do this to her, would he allow what's happened to her to happen to anyone? I hope I'm forgiven if there is a God because—because for the first time in my life I don't believe there is."

"Did she tell you which people were nice to her, Mr. Pisula?" Balzic asked.

"Yes. There was a girl, a Pat something. Patricia—"

"Keim?"

"Yes. She said she was very nice to her. Very friendly."

Balzic and Johnson exchanged frowns, remembering too clearly Patricia Keim's indifference to Janet Pisula.

"Mr. Pisula," Johnson said, "were you told what happened?"

Pisula nodded and then started to cry again. In a moment he

stopped and blew his nose. "Do you know, she was so beautiful when she was a child. She was my brother's. So beautiful . . ."

"What happened?"

"To my brother?"

Balzic nodded.

"An accident. She was seven. She was in the back seat. They were out for a drive. He'd just bought a new Ford. My God, was he proud. Their first time in that car. The next thing I know, a state police standing at the door. Just like tonight . . . she was brilliant, you know that? They had her tested when she was four. When she was four, she could add three-figure numbers in her head. She could read—and nobody taught her! They put her in kindergarten when she was four, and when she was five, they put her in second grade. The nuns did that. My brother and his wife, they were against it. They wanted her to stay with her own age, but the nuns insisted. And the nuns were right to do that. She was brilliant . . . and then they went for a drive. Some son of a—that idiot, passing a truck on a hill . . . my brother hit a utility pole. They were both dead. My sister-in-law instantly, they said. My brother, that night. . . ."

"Janet?"

"My wife and I, we—we couldn't have children . . . you're not supposed to want what your brother has, I know, but we wanted that little girl. The only envy I had for my brother . . . and then we got her. But how we got her, my God. In a coma for two months, brain surgery, and then, never again the same. How could it? But wasn't that enough? How much torture does God allow in one life?"

Johnson went for a cup of water. Balzic lit a cigarette and looked at the floor.

"And then he came to see her. The day after she regained consciousness. He'd been calling every day. The nurses told us.

And then he walked in, just like that, and you know what he said to her? He looked at her for a long time, just looked at her, and then he said, 'You should've died.' Just like that. And then he turned around and walked out . . . it was eight months before Janet said a word, two more months in the hospital, six months at home, and we were sitting down to eat, and she said—the first words in ten months—she said, 'Why did he say that to me?' Then she just played with her food. And what could we say to her, why that—that idiot, why he would even want to say anything at all?"

"Who was he, Mr. Pisula?"

"The driver of the other car, the one that passed that truck. A punk! The only time in my life I ever felt as though I could actually kill somebody myself. All wasted thoughts . . ."

"Why wasted?"

"Because he did it for me. Drove his car off a bridge—that same night. I didn't know until the next day even who he was. The police told us. I guess they thought they were doing us a favor."

"When you say that same night, you mean the night he came to the hospital?"

"Yes, yes."

"And Janet never got over that?"

"Never. It wasn't only the brain damage, it was that, you see? What possessed him to say that? Couldn't he realize what that would do to her? . . . I guess not."

"Did Janet know about the other driver?" Balzic asked. "I mean, did she know he'd killed himself?"

Pisula shook his head. "She never heard it from Ann or me. If she heard it from somebody else, I can't say. I know she never talked about any of it again—not with us anyway."

"Uh, Mr. Pisula, didn't she ever talk to anybody about it?"

Balzic asked. "I mean, didn't you think it was a good idea for her to talk to somebody about it?"

"A psychiatrist you mean? Sure. A couple of them. Oh, I don't know what they talked about with her. Not very much, I know that. Because they all said the same thing. All they wanted to do was talk about the brain damage. They talked about percentages. They said we'd have to learn to accept things as they were, that she would never be any better. I thought I would go crazy talking to them when they talked like that. I didn't understand—I still don't—how knowing a figure could make a difference. They talked like her mind was an adding machine, like a couple keys were broke and everybody would just have to go on adding, but without those keys. It didn't make sense to me . . . she was scared to death of them anyway . . . but I never thought the injury was as bad as what that punk said to her. She didn't have trouble taking care of herself. It was only in school that it showed up. She became average, a little below. From brilliant to average, from skipping grades to just keeping up. And she worked very hard. We never pressured her—Ann or me. We just wanted her to have some happiness—wasn't she entitled?"

"But she had trouble getting along with people?"

"With people? My God, yes. She was terrified of strangers. For a long time she wouldn't even go shopping with us. Only to school and then home. Then, little by little, she'd go out at night with us, but she wouldn't sit in the back seat. She'd sit right between us, and we could feel how tense she was all the while the car was moving. Then, when we were in the stores, she'd stay so close to Ann and me that sometimes we'd trip over each other's feet. She was in high school before she'd go anywhere without us. Even then it was only with Francey—my God, what'll this do to her?"

"Who's Francey?"

"Her friend. Oh my God, I can't tell her . . . I have to."

"Who is she, Mr. Pisula?"

"Francey—Frances Milocky. Our neighbor's daughter. She goes to Penn State. More than anyone, she's responsible for Janet coming out of herself. My God!"

"What's the matter?"

Pisula's body quivered as a chill racked him. "She's the one, she persuaded Janet to come here. Janet wouldn't have done it if Francey hadn't convinced her she could do it. Oh, God, what will this do to her . . ."

"She's in school now? At Penn State you said?" Balzic took out his notebook and wrote the name and address as Pisula gave it to him.

"Are you going to tell her?" Pisula asked.

"If you'd rather we did."

"Please. I don't think . . ."

"Did they keep in touch with one another?"

"Oh yes. They wrote all the time. They were very close."

"Did Janet say anything to you or your wife about anybody bothering her? Did she say anything about any trouble she was having? With anybody, about anything."

"No. Only with the work in class."

"Anything in particular? Or was it just generally hard for her?"

"No. The thing I'm talking about happened last semester. In her English."

"Was her teacher's name Keenan?"

"Yes. Dr. Keenan. She didn't like him at all. She was very afraid of him. He talked loud. And she said he was very rude."

"She had trouble doing work for him, didn't she?" Balzic said. "I mean, I know that she barely got a passing grade from him."

"Yes. She got a D. She didn't know what he expected. She didn't know what she was supposed to do."

"Did she talk to you about that? I mean, did you suggest anything to her?"

"I told her to take the course from another teacher. But that wasn't my idea. I didn't know you could do that. I never went to college. Francey told me to tell her that. And Francey told her too. And so she did. This semester she was in a Mr., a Mr., my God, I can't even think of his name."

"Farrell?"

"That's him. She liked him. She said she got along very well with him. She said he was very understanding. Nothing like the other one, that Keenan."

"And she never talked about having problems like that again?"

"No. Oh well, she had problems. But we knew what those were. Like her shorthand course. She used to worry that she couldn't keep up with the others, but I told her, my God, don't worry about that. Do the best you can. We have girls in our office making four hundred dollars a month, and they can't take shorthand at all. And their typing is terrible. And she could type very well. I said that's all you need. Don't worry. But she worried . . ."

"You said you knew what her other problems were," Johnson said. "What were they, aside from the one you just mentioned."

"Well, mostly the big problem. Coming out of herself, getting over that mess with the accident. . . . I remember she called us one night, and she said she was sick. And when I asked her how, she said it was because another girl got hit in the nose in her gym class, and the girl's nose started to bleed, and Janet said she passed out. And I said there was nothing wrong with that if she felt okay then. She said she did, so I wanted to know what was wrong, and all she could say was, 'Mommy, mommy.' She sounded awful. Just like a little girl. And it took me a couple minutes to figure it out, that she must've seen her mother like that in the car. . . . I asked her if she wanted me to come to be with her, but she said she was all right. She just had to tell somebody. And that was the only time she ever said anything about the accident . . ."

Balzic blew out a heavy sigh and wished that Toni Rosario was there to hear this.

"See," Pisula said, suddenly very animated, "I was convinced then that she had never been as badly injured as those doctors had said. Because if she had been hurt that bad, that would've meant to me that the coma she was in began in the car, that she had been knocked unconscious in the collision. But if she has a memory of seeing her mother's face with blood on it, maybe coming out of her nose, then . . ." His voice faded and he became still.

"Are the doctors who worked on her still around?" Balzic said.

"No. The one who did the surgery, Henderson, he's dead. He died years ago. The others, I'd have to look up their names in my records. But they were all old men then."

"Anything else, Mr. Pisula? Anything at all, anything she said about anybody?"

Pisula shook his head and closed his eyes. "My God," he cried out, "if there was anything, don't you think I'd tell you!"

"Easy, Mr. Pisula, easy," Johnson said. "That's enough questions. There's just one more thing, and God knows I hate to do it to you, but it has to be done." Johnson turned to Balzic, but Balzic shook his head and stepped quickly to the water cooler, still shaking his head as he filled a paper cup and drank. Nothing in the world could have made him go along with that man to watch as he identified the body. The sound of hell was the voices of the next of kin in a morgue—Balzic knew that in his bones. And he did not need to be reminded of it again tonight. . . .

Balzic hunched himself into a corner of Johnson's office, the letters of Frances Milocky to Janet Pisula in his lap, smoking and sipping coffee, trying to piece together the picture he was getting of Janet Pisula. All the pieces said "victim," but Balzic was uncomfortable with the pieces. Yet the more he read Frances Milocky's letters—there were thirty-one of them—the more sure he was that the pieces would form the pattern of a victim than that they would not.

What contributed most to the pattern of a victim he was getting about Janet Pisula was that of the first ten letters to her from the Milocky girl every one closed with the same words: "A lively understandable spirit once entertained you. It will come again. Be still. Wait." The words were always the same, always in quotation marks, and always the last words above Frances Milocky's signature.

Balzic went through those ten letters again before he got any clear thought why those words should not only add to the pieces making a picture of a victim but should actually become the frame for it. It was the advice of a doctor to a patient. "Be still. Wait." Be patient. A patient, Balzic had heard from a doctor once while he waited to visit someone in a hospital, was called a patient because he was waiting for someone else to heal him. "That's why doctors make such lousy patients," the doctor had said. "They have no patience—not that kind anyway." The doctor had not smiled when he said it. Balzic tried to think of that doctor's name, but knew that he had never known it. His recollection was part of a conversation between strangers. . . .

In the eleventh letter, the same words in quotation appeared, but were followed by more, these set down in the form of poetry:

The world is for the living. Who are they?
We dared the dark to reach the white and warm.
She was the wind when wind was in my way;
Alive at noon, I perished in her form.
Who rise from flesh to spirit know the fall;
The word outleaps the world, and light is all.

"Jesus Christ," Balzic said, and the three men from Johnson's squad who were going through the rest of Janet Pisula's papers and notebooks looked up expectantly.

"Find something?" one of them asked.

"Nah," Balzic replied. "Just some stuff my daughters would call real heavy."

Of the letters Balzic had read, most contained the usual exchange of information he expected to find: descriptions of Frances Milocky's room, her roommates, complaints about her roommates' bathroom habits, harangues about studying to be done, books to be read, assignments to do, grades anticipated and received—everything except even the most casual reference to a boy. Frances Milocky seemed scrupulous about avoiding it.

It wasn't until the twelfth letter that a man was even mentioned, and that was a brief paragraph about how considerate Janet's uncle ". . . had been to think of it." Whatever "it" is, Balzic thought.

In the thirteenth letter, dated December 1, near the end Frances Milocky wrote: "I hope you'll take my advice. Just don't even think about the worm. Any man who has to use that tactic to motivate anybody has got to be warped. Do what we talked about over Thanksgiving. Do it please, Janet. For your sake. I give you my word, he'll never know the difference." Then came the line about the "lively understandable spirit," followed by some of the poetry from the earlier letter.

In the fourteenth letter, dated December 9: "Quit feeling guilty about doing that, Jan. There's no need to. Really. People do that here all the time. They pay lots more than you're paying, believe me. There are people here who make a living from it. It's as much a part of this place as pot. Nobody even wonders about whether it's done; all they wonder about is whether they should do it, though of course they also wonder if they can afford it. But for God's sake, quit feeling guilty about it. Next semester you'll be all right, as soon as you're out of Keenan's class. Just be sure to get to registration early enough so you won't have to take him again. Registration here is pure chaos. It can't possibly be as bad where you are."

In the fifteenth, dated December 14: "See, dummy, what did I tell you? I told you he wouldn't know the difference. What counts is you still got the grade. And what do you care anyway? Besides, if he had suspected something, don't you think he would've called you in and said something about it? He probably thinks he made some kind of giant progress. From the way you talked about him Thanksgiving, I'd say he has to have the biggest ego in the western world. He's probably telling all his colleagues (don't you just hate it when they call each other that?) that he's really Super Teacher. Can't you just see him? He goes into the faculty-lounge john, rips off his corduroy jacket, and comes flying out in a cap and gown with a big red S on his chest—Super Prof! I'll bet he wears bikini shorts."

I wouldn't take twenty to one against that, Balzic thought.

The sixteenth, dated December 18: "Just a note, Jan. I have to hurry. Going to Scranton with Diane. See you on the 20th."

It was the first letter in which the line about the "lively under-standable spirit" and the poetry did not appear.

In the seventeenth, dated January 8: "Jan, why do you do that to yourself? I mean, really, there's no point. It's such a waste. If you hadn't done it, you would've flunked for certain. And what difference does it make to Uncle Mike? How can he be hurt by something he doesn't know? And who's going to tell him? You? Do you think I would? Jan, only three people know, and two of us don't want to hurt anyone, especially not Uncle Mike, and why would the third person have any reason? Everything he does depends on maintaining your confidence, otherwise he's out of business. Sometimes you make me so crazy I could scream. Just please put those dumb ideas out of your head because, Jan, please believe me, they are dumb. You've been paranoid long enough. We both know that, and we both know you had every right to feel paranoid. But not about this. There just isn't any reason. How many times have we talked about how your paranoia slips over? We've talked about it too many times to count, and I really thought you were getting over that part of it. Maybe you'll never get over all of it, but at least tell yourself that the original reason for it was valid but that all the others aren't. I know. It sounds so easy for me to say, but I can't help it. It is easy for me to say because for me it is easy. Please don't take this wrong, okay? Remember? 'Who rise from flesh to spirit know the fall'? Think about it some more, okay?"

The eighteenth through the twenty-fifth letters contained nothing out of the ordinary. Everything in them was usual, cordial gossip. In the twenty-sixth, dated April 11, Balzic found this postscript: "As for what we talked about last week, all I can do is repeat what I said. Just keep thinking that you only have to put up with him a couple more weeks."

In the twenty-seventh, dated April 17, again in a postscript:

"As for you know who, you have to learn to deal with people like that, Jan, that's all there is to it. I know it can get icky, and I'm not half as hung up about this sort of thing as you are. But you have to get tough. Otherwise, people will be stepping on your mind forever. You've been stepped on enough. Come on, Jan, toughen up!"

The twenty-eighth through the thirtieth letters were gossipy, girlish, drifting occasionally into something about school-work that was bothering one or the other but with no sense of urgency. All ended with some poetry. The thirty-first, and last, letter wasn't that much different. There was just one short passage referring to ". . . you know who." Frances Milocky wrote: "Some people give you things and if you aren't careful you'll give everything you have to them. But you owe him nothing!!!! Don't forget that, okay?"

Balzic put aside the stack of letters, took out his notebook, and copied from one of them all of the poetry. Then he put the letters in a manila envelope, marked them, and handed the envelope to one of the three troopers still going through the rest of the papers. He stretched, stifled a yawn, and looked at his watch. Two A.M. He felt suddenly very tired, and he thought the best thing he could do was go home and go to bed. He started out of the office but heard footsteps coming down the hall and waited, leaning against the doorframe.

Johnson came in, looking drained, shaking his head.

"How'd it go, Walk?"

"Shit, Grimes lifted the sheet and that poor bastard went down like somebody hit him in the head with a brick."

"Is he okay?"

"Hell, I thought he had a heart attack, but they got him into intensive care and wired him up to one of those EKGs. The head nurse said it looked normal, but they're still going to keep him until tomorrow anyway . . . man, those nurses in that outfit are really something. You know how old the head nurse was? Twenty-six, and she looked like seventeen."

"Yeah, I know. That's some group they got there. All of them are young. Did, uh, Grimes say anything else?"

"He pegged it down to last Wednesday night. That's as close as he can get."

"You get anything else out of Pisula?"

"Enough. 'Course I didn't want to pressure him. He did tell me how much money he gave the girl. Twenty-five a week, which I thought was a hell of a lot until he said she had to eat out every meal. He also said she went home every weekend—"

"Couldn't have been."

"What do you mean?"

"She couldn't have gone home every weekend, otherwise why didn't they say something last weekend—when she didn't show?"

"You didn't let me finish," Johnson said.

"Oh. So go ahead."

"The reason she didn't go home last weekend was because she told him she wanted to study for her finals. As a matter of fact, she called home last Wednesday afternoon and told him she'd decided to stay the weekend, which would have been her first, and he said he was happy about it. He said he had it measured how well she was getting along by how often she called home. The first month he said she called every day, sometimes twice. Then, he said, little by little, she got to the point where she was only calling once a week. He also said he and his wife made it a point never to call her. And that's about all I got out of him."

"Well," Balzic said, "there's some letters in that envelope on your desk you ought to read. From that Milocky girl who's supposed to be her best friend. There's a guy in it, that's for sure.

But no names. Just Keenan's a couple times, and unless I read them all wrong, he's not the guy." That said, he started for the door. He suddenly had to get out of the room. He couldn't say why, and he didn't want to stand around explaining.

"Where you going?" Johnson said.

"I think I'll hit Muscotti's for a couple cold ones, and then I'm going home. My ass is draggin.'"

"Don't you want to go through the rest of her stuff?"

"What for? Christ, you got three guys doing that. What do you want me around for?"

"I just thought you might want to stick around. What's the matter? You look edgy as hell."

"I don't know. Maybe all this efficiency scares me. It's hot. I'm tired. You don't do any good when you're beat. I'll call you in the morning." He left before Johnson could say anything else.

He wasn't sure at first what had driven him out of Johnson's office. All he knew was that he had to get out. He sat in his cruiser for a couple of minutes before turning the ignition, telling himself that he probably shouldn't look too carefully at the cause of his leaving the way he did, but he knew that something drove him out and that that something ought to be looked at.

He was halfway to Muscotti's when he got down to it, and he had to laugh out loud at himself. He knew he'd have to be careful who he told about it, otherwise he might have to turn in his shield and resign from the Fraternal Order of Police. There was only one way for him to say it honestly: he really could not stand being around Pennsylvania State Police.

He knew it didn't have anything to do with any one of them or with anything that any one of them had ever done to him. He took them as they came. It had to do with the gray color of their uniforms and the words that came to mind when he tried to describe that color. Anybody else might simply have said their shirts were light gray and their trousers dark gray. But Balzic thought of their shirts as being the color of shale and their trousers the color of slate. Shale and slate—the words a coal miner would use to describe them. No wonder he could not be around them for long. . . .

Inside Muscotti's, Albert Margiotti, Dom Muscotti's son-in-law, was tending the bar and drawing a beer for Father Manazo who sat in his poker clothes massaging his temples.

"S'matter, Father," Balzic said, "little early for you to be out of the game. It's not even quarter after two."

"I have a headache, Mario. I think it's my sinus. How are you?"

"Okay, I guess. That beer's not going to help your head."

"Naturally not," the priest said.

"Then you—"

The priest swiveled around on his stool and held up his hands. "Mario, please. A homily from you—as much as I like you and you know I do—but please, no homiletics. I'm drinking this beer out of spite for my head. Every man is entitled to spite himself once in a while, ridiculous as it may seem, if for no other reason than just to remind himself at times that he is ridiculous."

"Wow," Balzic said, shaking his hand limply from the wrist with the fingers together. "Give me a beer, Albert. And I got the Father's."

Albert put his hands on the bar and looked at his shoes. "Hey, Mario, uh, Dom asked me to ask you about your tab."

"Ask me about my what?"

"Uh, your tab, Mario—and hey, Mario, please don't come down on me, okay? You know I don't even like this job. I'm just helping the old man out, and if he tells me to ask somebody something, I ask, that's all. I don't want no grief over it. I got enough just being here."

"Hey," Balzic said, leaning on the bar, "you tell that old friggin' Tuscan to ask that skin-head Calabrez who works daylight what he did with the thirty-seven-fifty I handed him Memorial Day morning? You got it?"

"I got it, Mario. Okay? Just remember, I'm just asking, that's all."

"And you remember I'm just telling."

"Mario, not so loud," Father Marrazzo said. "My head, remember?"

"Hey, Father, I don't mean to be loud, but goddammit I been drinking in this saloon since 1946, and since 1946 I been running a tab and I never walked him yet. I don't mind Vinnie ragging me about it. That's, a standing joke between him and me, but this ain't the first time Vinnie took my tab and played it six bucks around on a number. And Dom knows that. You get what I mean, Father? And I don't like Dom asking Albert to ask me. Dom wants to know, he knows who to ask. This go-through-your-relatives is strictly bullshit, Father."

"Mario. Please," the priest said, rubbing his nose with his index fingers.

"Okay, Father, okay. I'm done." He looked at Albert. "So what're you gonna do, Albert? Do I get a beer or not?"

Albert drew the beer and set it in front of Balzic and then went to a cigar box under the cash register and wrote some figures on a piece of paper taken from the box.

"Thank you, Albert. How's your wife?"

"She's okay. Feeling a lot better."

"Good. Glad to hear that. Tell her I said hello."

Albert nodded. "Mario, you know—"

Balzic held up his hand. "Say no more. You're out of it."

Albert backed away and busied himself filling the beer coolers.

Balzic drank his beer without pause and motioned to Albert to draw another. He sipped the second and said, "I guess I should apologize, Father, for being loud, but to say it straight, I don't feel like it. I'm in a pretty foul mood—"

"I'll drink to that," the priest said.

"—from being around those state cops. Driving over here I was thinking about why I can't stay around them for very long. Yeah. Me. Who'd believe it? I have to work with them all the time. But I can only put up with being around them so long. And I know why, too. Which makes it even goofier."

"You are in a foul mood."

"The thing is, I'm not really. Most of the time I don't show anybody, that's all. I manage to keep it covered—usually. But sometimes things haunt you, and you can't keep them covered anymore. I mean, you can still cover them from other people, but you can't cover them from yourself. Like tonight, I was around all these state guys and I was looking at their uniforms, the color, and the words that kept coming into my head were shale and slate. Coal miners' words. And—ah, this is a load. You don't want to hear this."

"Go ahead and say it. Get it out."

"It's not important. Doesn't matter a damn to anybody."

"All right," the priest said. "I won't coax you."

Balzic stared at his beer, running his finger up and down the side of the glass. "We found a girl tonight, Father. Up in the Summer house. Been dead since last Wednesday. Strangled. And I'm really involved with that since maybe ten, ten-thirty, and all of a sudden, I can't stand to be in the same room with state guys. And one of them is a very good friend of mine. And you know why?"

The priest shook his head.

"My father is buried in Edna Number Two. Summer's mine."

"Your father?" the priest said. "You never said anything about that before. I don't know why that surprises me, but it does."

"I was three years old. I have no memory of him at all. None. I mean, except what my mother told me. And tonight, just being there, it's funny how I managed to put that out of my head until three or four hours later when I find myself in a room with four state guys . . . you know, my mother had a real fit when I told her I was going to be a cop. She wouldn't talk to me for two or three days. And I couldn't understand it. I kept asking her what was so bad about being a cop, and she wouldn't say a word. And when she finally did decide to talk to me again, the first thing she said—I'll never forget it—she said, 'If your father was here, he'd spit in your face and throw you out.' The look on her face, God . . ."

"Did he hate cops that much?"

"He was a miner, Father, and all he knew when he was in the mines was the Iron and Coal Police, the Pinkertons, and the Pennsylvania Constabulary. The Pennsylvania Constabulary became the state police. You know what the miners used to call them? The Black Cossacks. I thought my mother was exaggerating, but I did a lot of reading about it in the big Carnegie Library in Pittsburgh. There's another joke for you. I had to read about it in a library set up by one of the most heartless bastards who ever lived. But I found it, pictures and all. You ought to read about that time in this part of the state, Father. It's unbelievable.

"But anyway," Balzic went on, "it all came back to me tonight, and I thought I was going to choke in that room with those state guys. How's that? I felt like I was going to choke. That's what happened to the girl. What do the psychologists call that?"

"Identification? Is that what you mean?"

"Yeah. Something like that. The mind's a hell of a thing. Always surprises me the way it jumps around on you—course, I just might not be too bright."

"Oh, Mario, I doubt whether most people would have the honesty to question themselves about the way they were feeling. Now I understand."

"Understand what?"

"Why you reacted the way you did over your tab, over being asked to do something you'd already done."

"I'm not sure I want to know," Balzic said, motioning to Albert to draw two more beers. "Let's forget me for a while, Father. You read a lot, right?"

"That depends what you mean by a lot."

"Skip the modesty, Father. We both know you read a lot of books, especially psychology. Most of what I know about it, I got it first from you."

The priest shrugged.

"That girl we found tonight—another thing just came to me."

"What's that?"

"Why I made that identification with her."

"Why?"

"The more people I asked about her—except for her uncle— the less anybody could say about her. It's almost the same way with my old man and me. Lots of people knew him, but damn few can tell me anything that gives me a real feel of him, you know what I mean? It's the same with the girl . . . anyway, the thing I wanted to ask you about is this: she had a blank sheet of paper on her stomach. She's naked except for her panties, she's strangled with her brassiere, and according to the coroner, she was still a virgin. But what about that piece of paper, Father? What do you make of that?"

"I don't know. There's nothing on it? It's blank?"

"Nothing at all. And it was her paper. She also wasn't robbed. I'll tell you, it is the goddamndest thing I've ever come across."

"What do you make of it?"

Balzic shook his head. "I don't have the first idea. Neither does Johnson."

"Who? I don't know him."

"He's an old buddy of mine. He's a lieutenant in charge of CID until that asshole Minyon gets out of the hospital."

"What's wrong with him?"

"Ulcers or something. I wouldn't cry if he died."

The back door opened slowly, and, hat and tie askew, eyelids drooping, the left sleeve of his blue blazer ripped at the shoulder, Mo Valcanas shuffled in, singing in a way that only every third or fourth word could be heard.

"Holy hell," Balzic said. "What war'd you lose?"

"None of your goddamn business," Valcanas said. "Just direct me to the head. I have to speak to the ship's captain. Ship's company needs liberty."

"The head's the same place it's always been," Balzic said. "If you don't know where it is now, as many times as you've been in it."

"I'll be a sonuvabitch," Valcanas said. "Muscotti's. Didn't recognize the place. Now hell the how'd—how the hell'd I get here?"

"I hope you didn't drive."

"Who are you? Lou Harris? What do you care how I got here? Oh, it's you, Mario. Should've known. Well, pardon me while I relieve myself. In the meantime, before you arrest me for drunken walking, be advised to go pound sand. . . ."

Valcanas tottered toward the steps leading to the downstairs lavatory. The seat of his trousers and down to his knees was stained with blood.

"Hey, Mo," Balzic called out, "you got blood all over you."

"Wrong," Valcanas called up. "Usual for a cop. The blood is not *all* over me. It's restricted to the area immediate to and directly below my anus. My hemorrhoids cut loose. . . ."

Balzic looked at the priest and they shook their heads.

"What do you suppose happened to him?" Father Marrazo asked.

"Six'll get you five, Father, he smarted off at somebody a lot younger and a lot bigger. That's his style."

"With his intelligence—why?"

"My mother says some people have too much brains for their own good. That's Valcanas. He sees too good, hears too good, and he doesn't like what he sees or hears. That's about as near as I can figure him. Course, I don't try to figure him too much. I just take him the way he is and hope he stays out of trouble."

"It strikes me as a terrible waste."

"Oh, I don't know if I'd say that. I think he just doesn't like being sober—hell, what do I know? You want to know, ask him when he comes up. If he feels like it, he'll tell you. But if he doesn't, don't be offended if he tells you to take a flying trip to the moon."

"I won't be offended. I'll just feel sorry."

"Ouu, you better mean you'll be sorry for you. That's one thing I know he'll take your head off for, you give him a reason to think you feel sorry for him."

". . . oh say can you see, the Coast Guard at sea, through the fog, through the smog," Valcanas sang to the melody of the National Anthem as he weaved up the stairs and to a stool beside the priest.

"Don't stop now," Balzic said. "Let's hear the rest of it."

"I would," Valcanas said, grinning, "only I can't remember it. Innkeeper! A large whiskey and water. Canadian Club, if you please."

"Think you had enough, Mo," Albert said.

"I never met a bartender yet who could think. All they can do is add fast and everybody knows that doesn't take anything approaching thought. Pour the goddamn drink. I'll tell you when I've had enough."

Albert looked questioningly at Balzic.

"Go ahead," Balzic said. "Give it to him. He'll just go to sleep."

"Sleep, sleep. Valcanas hath murdered sleep . . . Valcanas doth murder sleep. Fuck you, sleep. You're dead. Bang. . . ."

"You, uh, read Shakespeare?" Father Marrazo said.

"Past tense. Read. I'm possibly the only person alive who ever finished *Timon of Athens* to the last hideous line. I thought I was going to learn something about Greeks. What a crock. And if that isn't masochism for you, give me a better example." Valcanas took out his billfold and, licking his thumb, stripped out a five. "That's the purest form of masochism I know—reading *Timon of Athens* to the last goddamn line. Hey, aren't you Father Marrazo?"

The priest said he was.

"Well, good, 'cause I have a question for you. And be honest. Don't quote me some goddamn papal bull."

The priest smiled and shook his head.

"What's so funny about that?"

"Nothing."

"Then what the hell are you laughing for?"

"I was thinking of something."

"There, Mario. See? An honest priest. He admits to thinking. Better be careful, Father. You'll get drummed out of the corps for doing that. Oh, you can do it. You just gotta be careful who you tell."

"So what is your question?"

"Oh. And remember. An honest answer. Did Jesus ever fool around with Mary Magdalene?"

"Aw come on, Mo," Balzic said.

"Stay out of it. You'd've been there, you'd've busted her for assignation, solicitation, and you'd've probably tried to trump up an attempt to commit sodomy. Shut up a minute. I want to hear what the priest has to say."

"You really expect me to answer you?" Father Marrazo said.

"I don't ask questions unless I expect an answer. Did he or didn't he?"

"Well, going on the evidence of the scripture, I would say no."

"Okay, then tell me this: do you think he wanted to?"

"That I can't say," the priest said, smiling.

"Well in that holy trinity he was supposed to be, one-third of him was man, right?"

"Yes."

"And men have desires, don't they?"

"Yes. I suppose most men do."

"All men, Father. All men. You guys are just experts in conning yourselves that you don't."

"Okay, okay," the priest said, laughing.

"Then answer me. Did he desire ol' Mary Mag or not?"

"I can't say."

"Well shit, man, what do you think? I mean, I just got the hell kicked out of me by some wop football player who didn't like my saying that Jesus had to have some eyes for Mary Mag, otherwise he wouldn't have been so damn quick to forgive her. Now, did I get the hell beat out of me for nothing?"

"I'm afraid you did."

"Why?"

"Because any answer would be conjectural. There's nothing written about it one way or the other."

"Then the only other explanation for his forgiving her was nothing but goddamn arrogance. Who the hell was he to forgive any woman for trying to earn her living?"

"Boy, you really are cranked up," Balzic said.

"A hell of a lot of satisfaction I'm getting out of you two," Valcanas said.

"Let's change the subject, okay?" Balzic said. "I got something I want to ask you, Mo. You read a lot—"

"I haven't read four books since Christmas."

"You read enough. I know that. So tell me. Why does somebody kill somebody and leave a blank piece of paper on her stomach? What's the message?"

"Do what?"

"Why would somebody strangle a girl, not rape her, not rob her, and then leave a blank piece of paper on her stomach?"

"Where the hell did you hear that? Did this actually happen or is this supposed to be hypothetical?"

"I wish it was hypothetical. We found her tonight. She's been dead at least nine days. Two people right across the hall from her and they didn't hear a peep."

"A piece of paper. With nothing on it?"

"Plain, ordinary typing paper. It belonged to the victim. And nothing on it."

Valcanas drained his glass and motioned to Albert to bring another drink. "That's the goddamndest thing I ever heard— oh, wait. Wait a minute. Right before Hemingway killed himself—the poor sonuvabitch—one of the last things he said to anybody, he was talking to his doctor. And he said something like, 'Doc, I can't make a sentence any more.' Something like that."

"So go ahead and make the connection," Balzic said.

"Well, he couldn't make a sentence. He couldn't write. He couldn't get it out of him. He couldn't get it on the page. And everytime you start, the page is always blank, right?"

"Right," Balzic said. "But he killed himself."

"Aw, come on, Mario. What the hell's suicide? It's self-murder.

And murder's murder. It all depends which way the gun's pointed."

"Okay. So what you're saying is, it was a writer who couldn't write."

"Well, hell, that's just a guess. I mean, there were lots of other reasons Hemingway killed himself. He was sick, his liver was shot. He'd just had a couple trips to the Mayo brothers' hotel. Shock treatments, that bit. But I'm just telling you the last thing he said to anybody before he did it. The connection to that and what you're talking about seems pretty obvious, that's all I'm saying."

"Uh-huh," Balzic said, taking out his notebook. "Well, here. Listen to this. I want to hear what you two think of this. 'The world is for the living. Who are they? We dared the dark to reach the white and warm. She was the wind when wind was in my way; alive at noon, I perished in her form. Who rise from flesh to spirit know the fall; the word outleaps the world, and light is all.'"

"What the hell is this," Valcanas grumbled. "I feel like I'm on some goddamn quiz show for crissake."

"Just tell me what you think of it," Balzic said.

"Are you asking me what I think of it, or you asking me what I think it means?"

"Both, I guess."

"Well I'll tell you what I think of it. I think it was written by somebody who's a bigger goddamn manic-depressive than I am—and that's going some," Valcanas said.

"Doesn't mean anything else to you?"

"What the fuck you want? I come in here all chopped up and you start reading things at me. Christ, I didn't even know I was here when I got here. Still don't."

"What about you, Father? What do you think?"

"I'd have to agree with Mo, at least partly. It certainly sounds like somebody had a very bad time of it and then pulled himself together a little too euphorically."

"I'll drink to that," Valcanas said. "What was that one part again—who rise from what to what?"

"'Who rise from flesh to spirit know the fall,'" Balzic read.

"Christ, that's a roller-coaster ride if I ever heard one. Even got the rhythm for it. Down up, down up, down up, Jesus. Where the hell'd you get that anyway?"

"I found it in a bunch of letters to the dead girl."

"Well, if somebody was trying to cheer her up, they sure picked some heavy artillery to do it with. Christ, I hear any more of that I'll have a relapse right here—what the hell are you doing making me think about crap like that anyway? All I wanted to do was stay fogged in. I didn't want to think about anything."

"You drink to avoid thinking?" Father Marrazo asked.

"Now you got it, padre. If you think, don't drink. If you drink, don't think. Christ, I should've been an ad man . . . have a Canadian Club adventure, go everywhere and never move off a bar stool. Walter Mitty was really a lush . . ."

"That reminds me of something," the priest said. "I remember reading about a study done by some psychiatrist that of all America's Nobel prize winners in literature, only one, Pearl Buck, wasn't a heavy drinker or an alcoholic. O'Neill, Sinclair Lewis, Hemingway, Steinbeck, and, oh, who was the other one?"

"Faulkner," Valcanas said. "Champion of them all. He made his own when he couldn't afford it. And that, padre, is true dedication to the pursuit of oblivion. Life, liberty, and the pursuit of oblivion. Liberty, equality, oblivion . . . up everybody's." That said, Valcanas drained his glass and tottered toward the door.

"Hey, Mo," Balzic called after him, "you're not going to drive, are you?"

"Hell, no. I'm going to my office. I have a cot in the cellar. Maybe there'll be an earthquake."

"Well throw your keys here then."

"Then how do I get into my office? Break a window? Then one of your clowns busts me for breaking and entering."

"Just your car keys."

"Oh, will you quit acting like somebody's goddamn mother. I told you I'm not driving for crissake. It's only two blocks from here. Since when do I have to listen to this horseshit—concern for my safety, Jesus . . ."

"I'm not concerned about your goddamn safety," Balzic said, but before he could say more, Valcanas had bounced off both door and frame and shuffled out.

Father Marrazo shook his head. "I still say it's a waste."

"If it's a waste, Father, I don't know what it's a waste of. I've seen him in court just slightly less juiced, making jerks out of assistant D.A.'s. Why don't you talk to one of them about it?"

Balzic left the priest sometime between three thirty and four, he didn't know exactly when. At home, he prowled back and forth between the living room and the kitchen, drinking cans of beer and eating a sandwich he'd made from crusty provolone, eating the sandwich to satisfy his hunger though it tasted flat as old provolone always does. He threw the last bit away, telling himself that it was a sin to waste food but a bigger sin to insult the stomach. By five thirty he was standing in the kitchen, looking out the window at the birds and squirrels waking, the birds bursting by his window like black darts and the squirrels rushing up and down the maples and diving from the sturdy, stiffer branches of the maples to the whippy, pencil-thin branches of the Chinese elm hedges Balzic used to plan to trim but never did. The hedges and the lilacs he'd planted in front of them formed a nearly opaque wall for most of the year, and what pleased Balzic most about that was that now the neighbors could only guess at how much he loafed. It had taken years for the hedges to grow as thick as they had, but it had only been in the last few years that Balzic felt he could loaf in peace without hearing later on from God knew who about how he stood around with his hands in his pockets when he should have been out rounding up the beasties and nasties and things that went bump.

The neighbors, Balzic snorted thoughtfully. He had to ask himself what their names were. He couldn't think of it. Yurkowski, Yurhoska, something like that. Good solid squares, scared shitless of niggers, dope heads, commies, rabid dogs, girls who went without brassieres, and people who made love with the lights on. His mother told him that about them. They were always complaining to his mother, and every once in a while, when she couldn't think up something new to put them off, she came to him and complained about them. The last time, a couple of months ago, he'd told his mother, "Ma, if I lock up everybody they're scared of, who's left? I'd have to lock up the world." To which his mother had replied impishly, "You big man, you no can do that?"

He turned away from the window and was startled to see his mother standing in the doorway of the kitchen. She was in her flannel gown, barefoot, her swollen ankles showing under the hem, her fingers over her mouth. She looked like she'd been standing there for some moments.

"Hey, kiddo, you still up. You sick?" Her voice was husky with sleep.

"I'm okay," he said. "What're you doing up?"

"I ask you first."

"I said I'm okay. Just didn't feel like sleeping. What about you?"

"Ahh, same thing. Ankles hurt like crazy. Back, too. I think I sleep on floor from now on. You want light?"

"Yeah. Go ahead, turn it on."

She flipped the switch by her shoulder and the overhead fluorescent hummed and then slowly filled the room with its bluish light. His mother sat at the kitchen table and rubbed one ankle with the other. "Hey, Mario," she said, squinting up at him, "what you decide?"

"About what?"

"Oh boy, you forget already?"

Balzic frowned. "I guess I did. What was I supposed to remember?"

"The cottage. You and Ruth and the girls and me. Next week. Tony's cottage. You forget to decide?"

"Oh that." Balzic sighed and rubbed his eyes. "Ma, I was thinking about it. I really was. But something came up and I quit thinking about it. It doesn't look like I'll be able to go anyway even if I wanted to."

"But you don't want. You still no like Tony. What for? What's he do for you? How come? Ruth very disappoint. Her only brother, Mario. All she got left. And you don't like."

"I know, Ma, I know. I can't help it. I just don't like the guy. I never did. I'm sorry he's all she got left out of her family. I wish she didn't have . . ." He let it hang there, wishing he hadn't said even the start of it.

"Oh, Mario. Not nice. Not nice what you was thinking."

Balzic looked away from her and yawned and rubbed his cheeks briskly. "I know it's not nice to think like that, Ma, but I can't help it."

"Mario, no kid around. What's he really do for you, you no like?"

"Ma, don't ask me, okay? It's embarrassing to talk about."

"So he really do something for you. Why you no tell Ruth? Why you never tell me before? Save lotsa trouble, kiddo."

"Ma, believe me, it would cause more trouble than it saves. I know what I'm talking about. Besides, I think it would probably be better if just you and Ruth and the kids went. The river doesn't really do all that much for me anyway."

"Oh, Mario, think how much cooler goin' to be there."

"All right, listen. I'll think about it some more, okay?"

"Hokay, I don't say nothing no more, but you got to say something to Ruth. She wants to know you goin' or not. Kids too. They looking forward, Mario. You know they goin' be swim all summer with that team. They no have more chance after next week." She stood, then winced and felt her lower back and had to hold the edge of the table to steady herself.

Balzic reached out to help her, but she shook her head.

"It's hokay," she said. "Just stiff. I think I go sleep on floor in living room. Don't step on me, hokay, kiddo? Good night."

He said good night and watched her go, still tilted forward from the waist, her feet flat on each step. He scratched his shoulders and wondered why he could not bring himself to tell her why he didn't want to spend a weekend at his brother-in-law's cottage on the Allegheny River. If she kept pressing him about it, he was going to have to tell her and Ruth something. They deserved some explanation, but he knew that when he finally got the nerve to give them one he was going to have to make it good. He arched his back and stared up at the ceiling. Shit, he thought. They'll see through anything I come up with. I'm going to have to lay it out, and is Ruth going to love that. Is she ever . . .

He tip-toed into the bedroom and started to undress. He was down to his socks and underwear when he thought to set the alarm. He set it for nine, hoping he'd hear it but knowing that he wouldn't, and then hoping that Ruth would know he'd set it for a reason and get him up.

He edged into bed beside her and stretched out. The last thing he remembered seeing on the insides of his eyelids was a blank piece of paper on the middle seat of an empty rowboat floating in slow circles past his brother-in-law's cottage. His mother and Ruth and Emily were standing in front of the cottage. Their faces were all confusion, the beginnings of panic. His brother-in-law was on the opposite shore, laughing obscenely and pointing at the skiff with his middle finger. Nobody seemed to know where Marie was; worse, nobody seemed to be doing anything about finding out where she was. Then he saw himself, standing on a sandbar in his underwear and socks. He had a pencil in his hand and he looked like he was trying to find something to write on. . . .

Balzic never heard the alarm. What he thought was the alarm was the phone ringing, and when he rolled over to shut the alarm and saw that it was a quarter after one, he bolted out of bed and hustled out to the kitchen phone, rubbing his eyes, scratching his belly, and swearing.

He picked up the phone and saw the note on the kitchen table in the same instant. He said, "Wait a minute," into the phone and picked up the note and read it. "Mario, I've taken Ma and the girls shopping. Didn't wake you when the alarm went off because you were really snoring and looked like you needed the sleep. Hope I didn't mess you up. Be back around three. Love, Ruth."

"I didn't get you up, did I?" Lieutenant Johnson said. "I mean, the last thing I want to do is fuck up your rest."

"Okay, okay. I'm up. So now what?"

"Well, listen, if you can tear yourself away from that bed,

I'd appreciate your help. I'm getting a blister from dialing the phone."

"What, you don't have people there?"

"Hell yes, I have people. Four of my people and three county guys. But they're all getting blisters too. We've only made about a hundred and three phone calls."

"About a hundred and three, huh," Balzic said. He sighed, coughed, brought up some phlegm, and leaned over and spit it into the kitchen sink, turning on the water in the same motion. "Listen. Give me twenty minutes. Just let me get cleaned up and get some coffee."

"Don't get too pretty. It's not your face I need. It's your finger. And we have all the coffee you want right here."

"You got my finger, friend," he said. "The middle one." He hung up before Johnson could retort, and twenty minutes later, with a patch of toilet paper congealed to a cut on his chin, he walked into the duty room of Troop A Barracks.

The air was heavy with cigar and cigarette smoke and the smell of both hot and cold coffee. Balzic nodded to the state men he knew by sight and to the three county detectives, Frank Rusa, John Dillman, and Tony Funari. Johnson appeared out of another office with both hands full of papers and started passing them around.

"Well," he said, "let's see if we can get the other twenty-seven." Seeing Balzic, he said, "Morning, sunshine. I thought you said you were going to get cleaned up."

"Save the smart mouth till somebody makes a movie about you," Balzic said. "Just tell me where's the coffee."

Johnson nodded to a table in the corner, and Balzic went to it and poured himself a cup from the large urn. "Well," he said, "what do you got?"

"I don't know whether you're ready for this," Johnson said.

"The thing is, I don't know if I'm ready for it. But here it is. There are one hundred and three people who were in one of four classes with the girl. So far, we've called all of them but we contacted, uh, seventy-six. Of the seventy-six—you hear this?—only fifteen remember ever even hearing her name. And of those fifteen, six were fairly sure they could put a name with a face. And of those six, only two ever remember talking to her, and those were the two who sat on either side of her in her shorthand class."

"And naturally," Balzic said, "all they remember talking about is what they had to do for the next class."

"Oh, one of them had a hell of a conversation with her one day. She asked her if she had an extra pen, and the Pisula girl said, and I quote, 'Yes.'"

"How the hell's that possible?" Balzic said, sipping his coffee.

"Well don't forget what her uncle said about her being scared stiff of strangers."

"Well shit, somebody had to say something to her. I mean, goddamn . . ."

"The newspaper still only come out six days here?" Johnson asked.

"Yeah. No Sundays. What'd you give them?"

"Everything I had, plus a plea for cooperation from anybody who might've seen anything. That was about ten this morning."

"That means it won't be in until Monday. Shit." Balzic sloshed his coffee around. "I been meaning to ask you. What's the word on the Milocky girl?"

"I got her mother around nine this morning. She expects her home sometime today, but she doesn't know when 'cause she's riding with somebody. The mother wasn't even sure when the girl's supposed to leave."

"You tell her mother?"

"I couldn't very well not tell her. People hear from a cop, they want to know something."

"Shit."

"What's the matter? Why the 'shit'?"

"Well, you read those letters. You heard what Pisula said. Those two were close. More than close. I hope she doesn't get the scrupulosities when she hears what happened and do something dumb."

"The what?"

"The scrupulosities. The guilties. That's what the priests call them when they get the people who run to confession after they crossed against a traffic light or got a parking ticket. Some people run to a priest, some run to a friend, some run to a psychiatrist, some of them just run."

"I thought you were the one who said not to think about all the things that could go wrong."

"Hey, Walk, she's it as far as I can see. If she can't tell us, nobody can. And when you get a situation like that, when you get two people and one of them doesn't have any trouble making it and the other one does, and the one who does breaks away from the one who doesn't—especially in this situation. The Milocky girl tells the other one to enroll here and then enrolls someplace else and then this happens—Christ, that's a dynamite situation. It might be that for the first time in their lives the situations are reversed."

"I'm not sure I follow," Johnson said.

"Well, all along, it's the Milocky girl who's the prop. She's holding up the Pisula girl. Now the Milocky girl needs a prop, and maybe the real jolt is going to be for her to find out she needs one. And then, what if there's nobody around? I mean, just for the simple reason she never thought she might need one, so she never looked for one—how about that?"

"Yeah, I see what you're getting at, but I don't necessarily think she's it for us. We still have a lot of lab reports to come in. We really don't know what we have."

"Which means you also don't know what you don't have either." Balzic chewed the inside of his lower lip and reached for a phone book.

"Who you looking up?"

"That Keenan. The one who's chairman of the English department."

"Why? I thought you said he was a real ballbuster."

"I'm not sure. I'd like to talk to him when he isn't half-juiced. Besides, I'm not cut out to sit around dialing phones. I hate fuckin' telephones. All you get is the voice. I want to see the face." Balzic found Malcolm Keenan's home address and made a note of it. He started for the door with a wave to Johnson.

"Well. Let me know," Johnson said.

"Yeah, sure," Balzic said, and went out to his cruiser and headed east to the Rocksburg city line and the beginning of Westfield Township.

Keenan's house, two-storied, covered with white aluminum, was situated on a sloping lot at the corner of Route 286 and Westfield Avenue. Though the township had recently annexed the land, the house and lot still had the complexion of the city, with sidewalks on two sides, an alley in the rear, a mailbox on a utility pole at the corner, and a fire hydrant in the middle of the block.

The house was old and boxy. Fifty years earlier it might have been built by one of Rocksburg's more prosperous businessmen; now, the white aluminum siding made it appear prim at the same time the taped window in the storm door made it appear as though the owners were indifferent to property. Balzic was reminded immediately of Keenan spilling the last drops of a drink on his corduroy jacket.

Balzic knocked on the storm door and was greeted by a large, collie-like mongrel which had been sleeping on the other side of the door and could not make up its mind whether to bark an alarm or wag its tail. It did both.

The door let into the kitchen, and from around a corner appeared a woman Balzic recalled seeing at the party at Dr. Beverley's house, the woman in the very short silver lamé dress.

She spoke through the screened upper third of the door. "Yes?" Before Balzic could reply she said, "Oh, it's you."

"Yes, it's me. Your husband here? I'd like to talk to him."

She hesitated, then said, "Won't you come in." The voice was Southern, possibly from North or South Carolina. She held the door open for Balzic and reached for the dog's collar to pull it back. "She'll jump all over you," she said, smiling nervously first at the dog and then at Balzic.

"As long as she jumps friendly, I don't mind."

"Oh my Lord, yes. She's spoiled rotten and thinks everybody who comes, comes just to see her. Won't you sit down? May I get you something cool to drink before I tell Mal you're here?"

Balzic sat and let the dog sniff at his shoes and legs. "A glass of water would be fine."

Balzic watched Mrs. Keenan moving from cupboard to refrigerator to sink. She was taller than Balzic had remembered, and like many tall women she tended to slouch. She seemed to be moving quickly, but for some reason Balzic couldn't figure she also seemed to be taking a long time to get him the glass of water. When Malcolm Keenan appeared around the corner, Balzic thought he understood. Keenan was nearly as drunk as he'd been when Balzic met him at the door of the Beverleys' house, and Mrs. Keenan was doing her best to avoid looking at him. When she set the glass of water in front of Balzic, she didn't look at Balzic either.

"Yesss?" Keenan said, scowling as though he'd been inter-rupted in the middle of something extremely important.

"Sorry to bother you," Balzic said and was cut short.

"You have already bothered me," Keenan said.

"Mal!" Mrs. Keenan said.

"Is he a friend of yours, or am I not permitted to know that?" Keenan said, breathing deeply twice and trying not to weave.

"It's the chief of police, Mal. You talked to him last night. At Some length. About a very serious thing—or don't you remember that either?"

Keenan focused on Balzic and seemed to make the associa-tion and then broke into a loud, staccato laugh, throwing back his head. "Surely," he said. "I was just rehearsing."

"Rehearsing?" Balzic said, watching their faces. Mrs. Keenan looked on the edge of tears, though whether it was from anger or humiliation Balzic couldn't guess. Probably both. Keenan tried to look sincere but could not bring it off. He excused himself, disappeared around the corner, and returned, rattling ice cubes in a tumbler. He opened a cabinet under the sink, took out a bottle of Scotch, and poured himself a couple of inches. Mrs. Keenan winced at the amount and then said quickly, "I think I'll leave you two alone."

"It isn't necessary," Balzic said.

"Oh but it is," she said. She patted her thigh twice and said, "Come on, Keenie." The mongrel lurched away from Balzic's feet and trotted after her. Before she went around the corner, she fired a look of reproach at her husband which seemed to amuse him.

"Women," Keenan said, drawing up another stool and settling uneasily onto it. He shrugged and said, "You are aware of course of what Freud said near the end of his life."

"No. Afraid not."

"He said that after forty years of working with women, he still had no idea what they wanted."

"I didn't know that."

"Neither did he," Keenan said, bursting into that staccato laugh.

Balzic let that go and said, "Uh, a little while ago you said you were rehearsing, and I asked you about it but you didn't answer."

"That's a very bad joke my wife doesn't appreciate. I use it whenever I think she is about to reprove me. I tell her that I am rehearsing for my life which is going to begin its run next week." Keenan smiled wistfully. "It infuriates her."

Balzic had to laugh in spite of himself.

"What is it that brings you here, sir?"

"The same thing we talked about last night."

"Well, sir, I have told you all I know about that girl. It was little enough, but I know no more."

"I didn't come here thinking you knew any more. I just came to have some things cleared up."

"Such as?"

"For one thing, last night you seemed pretty sure she wasn't doing her own work, and I'd like to know the reason you're so sure of that."

"Sir, I have been teaching for eleven years. Four at the University of Pittsburgh as a teaching assistant while I did my graduate work, four at Slippery Rock, and the last three here. One just gets a feel for such things."

"Yeah, well, I can understand that, but, uh, exactly how does one get this feel?"

"Aha! A man in search of cement."

"Cement?"

"Surely. Concrete, cement, the hard. As opposed to the abstract, the nebulous, the soft. You want water, not merely rain. You want the it, as in it is raining."

"Okay," Balzic said. "As long as it's about the Pisula girl, you can call it whatever you want."

Keenan made a humming sound and closed his eyes. "Let me think how to put this," he said, opening his eyes. "In a sentence, sir, the girl's prose took a quantum jump that was simply extraordinary."

"You lost me with that jump, what was it?"

"Quantum. A mathematical premise. The promise of arithmetic. Her words took the leap of a dwarf who suddenly realized his dream of becoming the Jolly Green Giant. It was impossible for me not to notice."

"So did you ask her about it?"

"No. As a matter of form, I complimented her on her jump."

"Even though you were pretty sure it was faked?"

"Even though. Surely. I mean, something must be said for the initiative to cheat, if for no other reason than for the imagination it requires. No. Demands."

Balzic shook his head. "Somehow I get the feeling you could, uh, make cancer sound like a good deal."

"Ah, well, words are the call, and mind outleaps pen, all in all."

"What was that?"

Keenan gulped more Scotch. "What was what?"

"You said something about mind outleaps the pen."

"What I said was, 'Words are the call, and mind outleaps pen, all in all.'"

"Did somebody write that by any chance?"

"I did. But purely as an exercise in form. Purely exercise."

"Sounds familiar."

"It does?"

Balzic took out his notebook and thumbed through it until he found the poetry he'd copied from Frances Milocky's letters to Janet Pisula. "Yeah, here it is. 'The word outleaps the world, and light is all.'"

"Theodore Roethke."

"Who?"

"Theodore Roethke. The sanest lunatic of the last forty years."

"What you're telling me is he's the guy who wrote that."

"Indeed, sir, he did. Between vacations to the mind sanctuaries. Or maybe during. But tell me, sir, what is a chief of police doing with the words of a poet in his notebook? Does that mean I can still hope for the age of the philosopher king to come upon us?"

"I don't know about that. I just know that what you said sounded familiar, that's all."

"Aaaaah, we're to cat and mouse, dog and cat, man and woman—is that it? You're to get me to confess that I'm familiar with Roethke. I'm dismayed, sir."

Balzic waited for Keenan to continue, but Keenan stood and poured himself another dose of Scotch. He returned to his stool, eased himself onto it, and took another long drink. Three full swallows.

"If it be treason, sir, to love poets," Keenan said, "then I am a traitor. Do with it what you will."

"Well, treason's a little out of my line. I'm just a cop here in Rocksburg. I don't work for the FBI."

"Your point, sir—" Keenan laughed uproariously. "Forgive me. What is your point?"

"I'm not really sure right now. Just tell me something. Is this, uh, this—"

"It's pronounced Ret-Key."

"Yeah, well, is he popular among college kids?"

"Popular? No, not popular. But his voice reaches those with certain ears."

"Uh-huh. Do you talk about him much in your classes?"

"I do. But that's because I have a singular affection for him. He has got me through more than one long night." Keenan closed his eyes and said, chanting in a voice like an aging priest's: "'This shaking keeps me steady. I should know. What falls away is always. And is near. I wake to sleep, and take my waking slow. I learn by going where I have to go.' That quatrain, sir, has got me through more than once."

Balzic studied Keenan's face for a moment. Keenan's eyes were still closed and his face was lifted slightly. Balzic turned to another page in his notebook and read, "'A lively understandable spirit once entertained you. It will come again. Be still. Wait.' Did the same guy write that, what I just read?"

Keenan nodded ponderously and opened his eyes slowly. "He did. It's from The Lost Son.'" Keenan closed one eye and opened the other very wide. "Again I must say, sir, I find this extraordinary. A chief of police with poetry in his notebook. Extraordinary."

"Not as extraordinary as you think," Balzic said. "But that's neither here nor there. Last night you said the Pisula girl shouldn't have even been in college, right?"

Keenan nodded slowly.

"You didn't think she was smart enough. She would've been better off waitin' tables someplace."

"Everybody would have been better off."

"Well a little while ago you said this Roethke wasn't popular, and I think you said something about him reaching those with certain ears—I think that's the way you put it."

"I did."

"So, uh, it sort of sounds like you think the people who hear him, the ones with those certain ears, it sounds like you think those people are pretty smart."

"Let me say this. I would not generally equate those with ears sufficient unto Roethke with undue intelligence, but I would say that they have made a wondrous beginning toward an awareness of the limits of their intelligence—yes, I would say that much."

"Okay, then tell me. How can you say what you just said on the one hand and then say on the other that the Pisula girl was dumb, how can you make that add up when I found all this poetry in her room?"

"You found those lines of Roethke's in her room?"

"That's right." Balzic was not about to say exactly where in her room he had found them.

"I'm truly perplexed," Keenan said. "Truly . . ." His chest came forward, his shoulders squared, he took several deep breaths, and he squinted unpleasantly. He started to speak, but before he could say anything, his wife appeared at the corner and said, "Mal, I would like to speak with you." Her teeth were clenched.

Keenan excused himself and followed his wife around the corner. For a minute their words were a jumble of harsh sounds, but then her voice rose and her words came clear.

". . . the third time this week, and I'll be damned if I am going to clean it up this time!"

"Patience, woman, patience—"

"Patience my behind! If the boy is sick he should be under a doctor's care. This is not a hospital. This is my home!"

"Control yourself. I will clean it up."

"I not only want it cleaned up. I want him out of here."

"I will ask him to leave."

"Ask him! Who does he think we are? Who do you think we are? Answer me, Mal. It is very important to me to know that at this moment."

"Lower your voice, woman, before you start to sound like a flaming hysteric."

"Do not tell me to lower my voice. And stop calling me woman. I do have a name. Or have you forgotten?"

"No, I have not."

"What is it, Mal? Tell me my name. Say it. I'd just like to hear you say it."

There was a long pause. Then Keenan said, "If you'll be good enough to get the mop and a bucket and some rags, I will go and clean the bathroom."

Mrs. Keenan strode heavily into the kitchen, her eyes brimming with tears, and she went from cabinet to broom closet to sink, gathering rags and sponge mop and filling a bucket with soapy water, taking everything around the corner. In a moment she was back, trying hard to compose herself.

"You'll have to excuse me," she said, taking a paper towel off a roll above the sink and wiping her eyes. "Last night he called me Keenie." A sob caught in her throat. "That's our dog," she said and bolted out of the kitchen.

Balzic chewed his lower lip, then stood and got more water. He was going to drink it and leave, but something told him to stay. He had an impulse to see who it was the Keenans were quarreling about.

He didn't have long to wait. He still had a third of a glass of water left when around the corner slouched a young man—he could have been anywhere from seventeen to twenty-five—wooly-haired, slender but unusually muscular, who was trying with hands and arms that would have fit a body forty or fifty pounds heavier and several inches taller to get a sleeveless denim jacket over a wrinkled and soiled tee-shirt.

His skin was pale, his eyes rheumy, and his nostrils wet. He looked as though he either suffered some allergy or had a cold or had recently been crying or vomiting. Because of the argument the Keenans had had, Balzic surmised the last.

"Afternoon," Balzic said.

"Is that a greeting, a declamation, or a policy position?" the boy-man said, staring, open-mouthed, at Balzic.

"Greeting."

"Then consider yourself greeted." The boy-man turned away from Balzic and looked thoughtfully at the cabinets. "Where the fuck're the glasses?" he asked, going from one cabinet to another.

"I think they're in this one," Balzic said, moving aside and pointing to the cabinet where he'd seen Mrs. Keenan get his.

"Hope you don't expect gratitude for that information," the boy-man said flatly, getting a glass and filling it.

"No."

"Good. Terrific. 'Cause I am philosophically opposed to that. I don't want anybody to get anything they don't expect." He drank the water, emptying the glass without pause, then filled it again.

Balzic couldn't avoid wondering about the disproportionate size of the boy-man's hands and arms. They were so large and obviously powerful that, taken with the boy-man's narrow body, they were grotesque.

The boy-man leaned against the sink and sipped more water. "So you're wondering about my hands, right?"

Balzic thought he had been more subtle. He nodded.

"To save your brain the sweat, my old man almost made the '36 Olympic gymnastics team. Almost, but not quite. So I was supposed to make the '60 or the '64 or the '68 or the '72 Olympic gymnastics team. That's what my old lady kept telling me my old man would've wanted. The thing was, I was never sure what my old man wanted 'cause he got himself killed saving the world from the Communist hordes in Korea. But that didn't matter to the old lady. She had me on the rings and parallel bars before I could walk." The boy-man finished his water and set the glass in the sink. "Satisfied?"

Balzic shrugged. "Are you?"

"Sat-is-fied. I like the first two syllables. Sat is. That's me. I's sat."

"I take it you don't do it anymore."

"You take that right, dad. You take it rickety-rackety right."

"What do you do?"

"You ask a lot of questions, man. You know that?"

"Yeah. I guess I do."

"Don't tell me. You're a cop."

"That's right."

"How about that. First test I've passed in a year."

"You a student?"

"No more I'm not." The boy-man canted his head. "And I'll tell you why, since I see you're gonna ask me. For the same reason I ain't going to the '72 Olympics. I got tired. I got tired doing giant swings, tired practicing dismounts, most of all I got tired trying to keep those fucking rings still."

"You'll have to explain that. I don't know very much about gymnastics."

"You never saw rings?"

"On television a couple of times I think."

"Well, they're just what they sound like. Two metal rings on the ends of a couple of straps. Somebody lifts you up to them and you start out with the rings as still as you can get them. Then you do your routine, man, whatever you do, but the important thing is you have to keep those rings still. Which ain't easy, man. I mean, they're on straps, you know? The more they move, the more points the judges knock off. And that's the way I felt about being little Stevie Student. Every time I took a test, every time I gave a paper in a seminar, I felt like I was just trying to keep those fucking rings still. And I just got tired, man. Sick and fucking tired. I got an ulcer as big as a silver dollar, man. That's how sick I got. And that's how sick I get."

"That why you throw up?"

"That's exactly why I throw up."

"And you don't bother to clean it up."

"You must've heard that little go-round between Keenan and his old lady."

"I couldn't help but hear it."

"So now you want to know why I don't clean it up, right? I mean, you throw up in somebody's house and make a mess, you're supposed to save the people the trouble and clean up after yourself, right?"

Balzic nodded.

"Man, nobody is going to save them their troubles. He wants to be a fucking bohemian and a college professor, chairman of the goddamn department no less—and he don't know how. And her, she wants to be married to the chairman of the department and a bohemian, in that order, plus she wants to be a liberated woman, and she don't know how to be that either. Meantime, they're both something straight out of a Romantic novel—no, Romantic Gothic. No. Romantic American Gothic. Percy and Mary Shelley moved to Rocksburg. . . . I figure I'm doing them a favor throwing up in their bathroom. They both need to look at a little puke with blood in it every once in a while. Just to let them know."

"Let them know what?"

"That it's there, man. That it smells. That it looks like nothing else. I go to my old lady's house every once in a while, and I barf in her bathroom, too."

"Just to let her know what it looks like?"

"Nah. She knows what it looks like. Just to remind her. She gave me the fucking ulcer. And him," the boy-man pointed at the ceiling, "the one mopping up up there, he just made it bigger. He took it from a quarter and turned it into a dollar."

"So you miss the toilet on purpose."

"Oh no, man. I make sure I hit part of the seat. To make it look like I tried. I mean, Christ, I could hit the toilet. I know when I got to heave, man. But every time I bend over, it looks like one of those goddamn rings, and I figure fuck it I know it's not going to move, but I know I'm not going to stay fucking still."

"What's your name by the way?"

"Segalovich. Anthony George Segalovich, the third. How do you like that—the third, no less. You can bet your hat, ass, and elbow there ain't goin' to be a fourth."

"Why not?"

"Are you kidding me? This line ends with me, dad. The old lady couldn't even come up with an original name for me. Who the fuck ever heard of a hunky with 'the third' after his name. Jesus . . ."

"How'd you meet Keenan?"

"I met him at Slippery Rock State College. Old Slimey Pebble. Yeah. And when I met him, I actually still thought I was happy. Shit, phys-ed major, two-time all-around gymnastics champ of Pennsylvania state colleges, third place NCAA College Division my freshman year, second place my sophomore year. Man, I was getting ready for the university division, the AAU, for those guys from Penn State and Southern Illinois . . . then I had to take an elective course. So I shut my eyes and put my finger in the catalogue and the next thing I know I'm in his poetry class. And the next thing I know, I'm not a phys-ed major anymore. Nah. I'm an English major. All because of Doctor Keenan."

"Now you come and throw up in his house and miss the can on purpose," Balzic said. "That's some switch."

"Right, man, right. And his old lady goes crazy, and he walks around, juiced out of his skull and making pronouncements which he thinks are going to move the world right off its axis, you know, except the trees just keep right on growing."

"A lot must've happened."

"I wised up is what happened. He wants me to keep the rings as still as my old lady did. He walks around saying, 'Thisss shaking keepssss me steady,' and all that shit, but he don't have the first idea how much you can shake trying to keep those rings steady, man. He's never been on those rings. Not once in his life. That's why I miss his toilet, man. And that's why I don't even think about cleaning it up. Fuck him. And fuck his old lady, too."

"Doesn't it ever get a little boring?" Balzic said after a moment.

"What?"

"Getting even."

Segalovich snorted and turned toward the door. "Doesn't it ever get a little boring for you, always playing question man? Doesn't that ever bore you?"

"Not as long as the answers are interesting," Balzic said, smiling.

"Then, question man, all you have to do is find answer man, and your life will be endlessly interesting. Stimulating even. See you around." Segalovich stepped out onto the porch and let the storm door bounce against its spring.

Okay, smart guy, Balzic said to himself, figure that monkey out. Figure Keenan out. Figure his wife out. Hell, Balzic thought with a grunt, how can you figure them when their dog doesn't even know what it's supposed to be.

He put his glass in the sink, ran hot water in it, and was starting for the door when Mrs. Keenan came into the kitchen.

"I'm sorry," she said.

"For what?"

"For losing control. I don't usually lose control like that. Usually I am very much in control."

"Well, we all slip once in a while."

She sat on the stool farthest away from Balzic and rested her forehead on her hand. "I presume you met the source of our— my irritation."

"Segalovich you mean. Yeah. Met him and listened to his story."

"Oh, he will do that. He will tell you his story."

"Listen, uh, I'd like to ask you something that isn't very pretty."

"If it's about him, not much is."

"Yeah. Well, uh, does your husband know Segalovich can't stand him?"

"Oh Lordy. My husband—" Mrs. Keenan laughed bitterly. "My husband not only knows. My husband actually thinks it's healthy. There is something affirmative, something positive, even in loathing, that is what my husband says. After all, if you cannot loathe properly, then you cannot admire properly either. And poets must know the depths of their loathing, else they will never know the heights of their admiring—that's what my husband says. Do you want to hear more?"

"That's enough. I get the drift. But what about you?"

"I thought that was fairly obvious."

"Well, your feelings are pretty obvious, but I'd like to know more than that."

"What can I tell you then? We met him—"

"He told me that."

"What do you want to know then?"

"A minute ago you said something about your husband

thinking that a poet ought to know his depths, and so forth. Am I right in thinking that because your husband puts up with Segalovich, that he, Segalovich, is also a poet?"

"Absolutely. Mal wouldn't have it any other way."

"Okay. So then how does he make his bread—his living?"

"That would take some telling."

"Well, you know, just briefly."

"I can't be brief about him. I know this isn't going to make any sense, but the reason I can't be brief is because I don't really know. I only have intimations of what he does. He used to go to school. He was working on his master's at Pitt, the main campus in Oakland. Then, he was doing all sorts of things: stealing, shoplifting, selling marijuana, selling practically anything anybody wanted to buy, writing papers for other students. Ostensibly, he had a job as a stock boy in one of the department stores in downtown Pittsburgh."

"What was that one thing you said—writing papers for other students? What's that mean?"

"Oh, that's a flourishing racket these days."

"Well I figured it was some kind of hustle, but exactly what kind of hustle is it?"

"Well, not having participated in such things when I was a student, I can only surmise."

"Go ahead."

"I imagine it's quite simple. A student's workload piles up, or he lets it pile up either because he can't or won't keep up, term papers come due, and when there is demand there is generally supply. I'm told it's a sellers' market."

"You mean one student pays another student to write his paper for him? Do his work for him, is that it?"

"That's what it comes down to. And from what I hear, it's gotten so far out of hand that it has even come up in the state legislature. Some university teachers are demanding that a law be passed making it some kind of crime."

"Yeah," Balzic said, "I remember hearing something about that, but since I didn't have anything to do with it, I didn't pay any attention to it. Well, let's get back to Segalovich. You know for a fact he did these things, or are you sure he wasn't maybe just bragging a little bit?"

"No, I don't know anything for a fact. And he most certainly does have a tendency to distort the truth in his favor—and that is being as polite as I can be."

"So you heard him talking about shoplifting and so on, but you're not sure he actually did these things."

"Well, I would have no way of being sure. All I know is that he hints at lots of things. And he always makes gross statements about himself. I've heard him say things like, oh, 'I have a bottomless well of evil,' or, 'I have an endless capacity for the corrupt.' They weren't about particular things he had done—or claims to have done. They were just general comments like that, which, I suppose because he disgusts me so much, I chose to believe that he is as capable of those things as he tries to make himself out to be."

"But you really don't think he's just bragging."

"He may be. It may be his way of playing the poet. On the other hand . . ."

"On the other hand what?"

"Well, he certainly has no qualms about freeloading here. He'll take anything he can get from Mal. Money, food, anything. And things that are not Mal's to give."

"You?"

"Yes. He tried that once. Mal went out somewhere, probably to get another bottle of Scotch. And he even tried to take that."

"Without the details—was he clumsy?"

She canted her head, looking half-surprised, half-pleased. "You were very sure of that, weren't you?"

"Just a guess," Balzic said.

"Well, boorish is a better word than clumsy. He disgusted me."

"Did he get a little rough?"

"For a moment I thought he was going to, but then Mal drove up. We both could hear the car. He just backed away and sat down."

"How long ago was this?"

"That was when we were at Slippery Rock. Five years ago at least. Now, he never comes near me."

"How long's he been here? I take it he's been living here, am I right?"

"This time he's been here only a little more than a week. I try not to think how long. Maybe it hasn't been quite that long. Maybe I just think it has. It seems a month."

"Where's he from?"

"Someplace near Pittsburgh. I really don't know. He claims he stays on the road—that's how he puts it."

"Do you know where he was before he came here?"

"Oh, he's back and forth. I don't really care to know so I never ask. I just sit and hope he's not planning to stay when he shows up."

"Okay, Mrs. Keenan, thank you very much. I might be talking to you again. Hope you don't mind."

"Mind? Lordy, nobody's—what I mean to say is, I'll be glad to assist in any way I can." She smiled and then blushed. "I presume all this has to do with last night."

"More or less. Anyway, I might have to talk to you or your husband again. Thanks again. And thanks for the water."

* * *

126

Balzic stepped off the porch into the brilliant sunlight. Coming from the subdued light of the Keenans' kitchen, he felt for a second as though someone had thrown sand in his eyes.

His cruiser was scorching—handles, seat, steering wheel—and opening the vents wide relieved little. He stopped at the first gas station he came to as much to get out of the car as to get gas. As an afterthought, he asked the attendant if there was a phone. The attendant motioned toward the inside, and Balzic went in, mopping his face and neck, and called his station.

"Rocksburg Police, Sergeant Stramsky speaking."

"Vic? Balzic. Where's Clemente? It's not four o'clock yet, is it?"

"It's five till three. Angelo's sick. His old lady called me this morning to take his shift for him."

"What's wrong with him?"

"She didn't say. All she said was they were getting ready to go to the doctor's. Said he didn't sleep last night."

"What, that's the second time this month. You know what I think? I think Angelo's starting to wonder whether he ought to retire."

"Hell, that ain't for six months yet."

"Ah, Angelo worries. He wonders and he worries. So. What's happening?"

"You really want to know?"

"On second thought, unless the Japs bombed the Rocksburg Boat Club I don't want to know nothing. Did my wife call?"

"No. Johnson did though. He said for you to go on up to Troop A."

"Okay, Vic. And listen, don't spend all that overtime on kolbassi. Buy a little cabbage too, you know."

"Funny man."

"Vic, don't hang up. There's about six or seven mobile homes coming through. Should be around quarter to four. See if Angelo set up escorts for them, and if he didn't, you take care of it."

"Front and rear?"

"You got it," Balzic said and hung up. He went back to his cruiser, paid the attendant, and drove to Troop A Barracks.

The county detectives had gone, and the duty room was empty except for the radio operator and a typist. The typist told Balzic that Johnson was in his office, and Balzic found him leaning back in his chair, toying thoughtfully with a pencil.

"So what's the good news?" Balzic said, straddling a chair.

"You're going to love this," Johnson said, closing his eyes and rolling his head from side to side to loosen a kink in his neck.

Balzic lit a cigarette and waited.

"The Milocky girl got the word and took off."

"Took off? For where?"

"Who knows. She came home about an hour ago, her mother told her what happened, she stewed around for a while, and then, according to her mother, she picked up a couple bags and just walked out. The old man was visiting Mrs. Pisula in the hospital and it took Mrs. Milocky a while to reach him."

"And?"

"They drove around looking for her and finally got around to the bus station. The nearest thing anybody could figure was that she caught a bus to Pittsburgh. Christ only knows where she'll go after that."

"You called the Pittsburgh police."

"Yeah, sure. Right before I called your station. About forty minutes ago. I don't know what the fuck they're doing. How long's it take to check the bus stations?"

"Beautiful," Balzic said. "I take it you decided she's it. The lab came up zilch, right?"

"Double zilch. Nothing from her fingernails, nothing from the floor, all the prints in the room were hers—except for the ones on the door which are yours—plus that one lousy smudge on the paper. Man, I read through all those letters and I have to agree with you. If anybody's going to tell us anything, it's going to be Miss Milocky."

"How about the rest of the people who were in her classes?"

"Nothing. I'll tell you, Mario, I never saw anybody as cut off from people as this girl was. She may as well have been in solitary for the last nine months. Nobody knows anything about her." Johnson shook his head wearily. "I got two men nosing around at the campus, but they just keep reporting back goose eggs. They've talked to the manager of the student union, the manager of the bookstore, librarians, janitors, everybody. Nobody can remember talking to her. It's fucking unbelievable. I was just sitting here thinking about it. Never mind that she got murdered. Imagine what her life was like, being that separated, that isolated. I'm really starting to feel for her uncle."

"Yeah, and the poor bastard thought she was coming out of it. Well, goddammit, Walk, she talked to somebody."

"Sure. But who? How about you, you get anything from that Keenan?"

"I got more out of his wife than I did out of him. All he wants to do is make jokes and drink."

"What did the wife say?"

"First of all, Keenan is certain the girl wasn't writing her own papers, then the wife tells me that's a pretty big hustle these days. She told me something I forgot, which was that it's getting so bad some professors are lobbying in Harrisburg to make it illegal."

"What is? What's the hustle?"

"Just what I said. There are people who are making money writing papers for other students."

"Oh, yeah, yeah. I remember hearing that in Harrisburg the last time I was there. But, shit, I always thought that was a hustle."

"It may have been, but apparently it's never been this widespread before. Anyway, you put that with the information in those letters and it's twenty to one that's what we're dealing with. What the hell else would she've been talking about? She kept on urging her to do it—where are those letters?"

Johnson nodded to the corner of his desk, and Balzic leaned over and picked up the manila envelope. He rooted through the letters until he found what he was looking for. "Here, listen to this one: 'Do what we talked about over Thanksgiving. Do it, please, Jan.' And this one. 'Quit feeling guilty about doing that, Jan. They pay lots more than you're paying for it, believe me. There are people here who make a living from it. It's as much a part of the place as pot. Nobody even wonders about whether it's done; all they wonder about is whether they should do it, though, of course, they also wonder if they can afford it.' See what I mean? I mean, what—"

"Hey, Mario, friend, buddy, compadre, I've read it," Johnson said, standing and stretching. "I've read them twice. The fact is, the only name mentioned in any of them is Keenan's, and nobody's going to tell me that the guy teaches a class and then writes papers for his students for money. Christ, that doesn't make any sense at all. Why do the work? If he wants money, why not a straight bribe for a good grade?"

"Agreed."

"Okay, so then where does that leave us?"

"Maybe they advertise."

"I'm ahead of you. One of the things I told my people down

on the campus was to check all the bulletin boards, see if there was anything that looked even remotely like a pitch."

"And?"

"Everything posted on the boards was ordered off on a memo from the president's office. The boards had to be cleared by the time the last exam was given yesterday. Seems they don't have too much space and they needed all they could get for information for the summer school."

"So it's in the garbage, right?"

"Right. And I already talked to the sanitation department—"

"Oh shit," Balzic said.

"Right. City ordinance number-who-knows says that all garbage must be buried in a landfill the same day it's collected. All of a sudden the whole fucking world gets efficient."

"Christ," Balzic said, "I'll lay a hundred against one if I wanted to go to summer school, if I wanted to do that today, I'd have to go to some dean's house to get the information. It wouldn't be on any goddamn bulletin board if I was looking to find out how to go about it. And if I don't put my garbage cans in exactly the right place, I can start a rat farm waiting for somebody to tell me why they didn't pick it up."

"Well, what the hell, suppose the guy we're looking for is in the business of writing papers. He couldn't make a living off a school as small as this one. He'd have to be working everywhere he can, right? I mean, there are a hell of a lot of colleges around here."

"Three big ones in Pittsburgh," Balzic said, "plus all the small ones. There gotta be twenty, twenty-five within fifty miles."

"So? We run them down. We don't have any choice. I'll—"

The phone rang then and Johnson picked it up.

"Speaking," he said and then said to Balzic, "It's Pittsburgh. Yeah, go ahead . . . Greyhound eastbound . . . Ocean City . . . yeah, certainly we'll get a mugshot . . . yeah, I'll put it out on our wire . . . hey, man, thank you. I'll take it from here." Johnson hung up. "That guy was something else. He tells me to make sure I get a mugshot and put it out. He must've just got promoted."

"They got her?"

"Yeppie. Ticket seller remembered her because she was very nervous and he asked her if she was all right, and she said no, because a very good friend of hers just died. She's on her way to Ocean City—well, you heard that. So, all I do is get the route and have her picked up. Christ, what could be easier?" Johnson smiled. "How's that for luck?"

"The last time I thought about it, I figured there were at least two kinds of luck."

"Hey, pessimist, look at it this way. If we miss her all the way to Philly, we just wake up the Jersey state people."

"As long as she goes where the ticket says."

"Why wouldn't she? You called her right before. You said it would be a dynamite situation if she found out she needed a prop as much as she thought the Pisula girl did. So? She just found out she needed one. And it looks like there's none around. So she's running where there is one. If she's half that predictable, she's going where the ticket says. I don't think there's any sweat."

"Your confidence in my ideas, lieutenant," Balzic said, "is enough to make a man think he still has a right to go to swimming pools."

"Do what?"

"You know, when you hit a certain age, the legs get a little whiter and the gut hangs and you get a little nervous being around all the young snappers. The ones with the flat bellies and the tight asses. You wonder how they see you."

"Mario, I didn't think you thought about those things anymore."

"Hey, are you kidding? The only time I go to the pool is to watch my daughters swim for the rec board team."

There was nothing to do now but wait. If Frances Milocky was on a Greyhound going to Ocean City, New Jersey, it was simple. A state cruiser would be waiting at one of the stops, if not one, then the next. Balzic knew Johnson knew how to coordinate things like this. It was what Johnson did best.

Still, Balzic fretted about it. Frances Milocky went to the largest university in the state. Unlike Janet Pisula, she had to have made many acquaintances. Balzic remembered the letter in which she wrote about going to Scranton with somebody for a weekend. Scranton was east. Suppose she changed her mind about going to Ocean City. Suppose she—ah, suppose, suppose, suppose, Balzic groused. I could sit here supposing until my ass turns to plaster and winds up on somebody's ceiling. Best thing for me to do is relieve Stramsky so he can eat. . . .

He drove to his own station, told Stramsky to take an hour off, and settled himself at the radio console. He found a deck of cards and started to lay out a game of solitaire, then snapped his fingers and went to a phone and dialed his home.

His wife answered. "Mario, where the hell are you?"

"Some hello I get. Where you think I am? At the station."

"Well, I wish you'd come home. I want to talk to you."

"You can't talk to me now? I could swear you were talking to me."

"Mario, don't get smart. This is important and I can't tell what you look like over the phone. I want to see you when I talk to you."

"Awww, you just want to look at my face. I like you, too."

"Mario—will you stop. This is serious. Your mother told me something, and I want to know what it's about. You been holding out on me."

"Holding out on you? About what?"

"About my brother, that's what. And don't play dumb. I know you."

"Listen, Ruth, I don't know what Ma told you," Balzic lied, knowing too well that she knew him. She didn't need to see his face to know when he was trying to con her.

"Listen, you," she said, "ever since I started talking about going to Tony's cottage, I can see something's wrong. And don't try to tell me you didn't say anything to your mother. 'Cause she told me something and I want to know the rest of it. If you have something against Tony I want to hear it. 'Cause I'm not going to spend a weekend with the two of you in that little place and not know there's a war going on behind my back."

"Ruth, listen. Maybe you're right. Maybe we ought to talk about this when we're looking at each other. You started out okay, but your tone's getting a little sharp, and if I told you over the phone, I think you're going to get madder than you should."

"Mario, is it that bad? Is he doing something illegal?"

"No, nothing like that Look. Give me some time to think how I want to say it, okay? And I promise, I won't hold out. I'll give you the whole story, okay?"

"Promise?"

"I promise. It may take me a couple days to figure how I want to say it, but you'll hear it."

"Okay," she said, her tone softer now. "But don't take too long, okay? If we're going, I'd like to have a couple days to get ready."

"You'll have time," he said. "So how's everybody?"

"The girls are all right. Ma's having one of her bad days. Her back's bothering her. But she doesn't want me fussing over her so it can't be too bad. Listen, when are you coming home?"

"I don't know. Something happened. I'll probably be here for a while. Maybe most of the night. Tomorrow, too."

"So when are we going to have this talk?"

"Will you quit worrying? I told you I'll tell you and I will. I just can't do it right now, okay?"

"Okay, Mario. I'll see you when you get here."

She hung up and Balzic let out a long sigh and cleared his throat. Whatever he told her would have to be said softly, with the right words. This was touchy. He was trying to think of his first words to Ruth when he finally got around to explaining to her what was really bothering him about her brother, talking to himself at first, and then whispering to hear how the words sounded. He thought for a moment he had the perfect way to approach it but lost the thought when he swiveled around and saw A.J. Scumaci standing on the other side of the counter. Balzic had not heard him come in.

Angelo Joseph Scumaci—A.J. to those who indulged him, Johnny Scum to those who didn't—his eyes wildly confessional, swayed from foot to foot, his battered black fedora going in eccentric circles in his arthritic hands.

"A.J., what the hell do you want? If you want to borrow some bread, say so, but save the stories. I don't want to hear anything."

"Mario Chief, I didn't mean to do it, honest to God, I didn't. I don't know what makes me do these things. I'm not right. Everybody knows that. I'm dangerous—"

"A.J., the only time you were ever dangerous was when you used to cook in Romeo's place." Balzic hung his head and laced his fingers and stretched his hands in front of him.

"I mean it," A.J. said. "I should be put away. I shouldn't be allowed to walk the streets. I murdered a girl and I should be put away for the rest of my natural life."

Balzic went through the lifting door in the counter and took A.J. by the arm and led him toward the door. "A.J., you never had a natural life and you're never going to have a natural life. Now get outta here. You want a free ride on the state, do what I told you a hundred times already. Go sign up for welfare. Now go. Out."

"Mario Chief, on my mother's soul I murdered a girl—"

"If you murdered all the girls you said you did, A.J., there wouldn't be a woman alive in Pennsylvania. Now please get outta here. Don't make me lose patience with you."

A.J. shuffled out, but turned around on the porch and stared glumly through the screen. "Mario Chief, could you please—"

"How much?"

"Two—a dollar would be plenty."

Balzic reached in his pocket, brought out some bills, and held up two dollars. A.J. opened the door far enough to get his arm through. He snatched the bills, jammed them into his hat, and pulled it down to his ears. "God bless you, Mario Chief. I won't forget this. You know me. A.J. never forgets nothing. A.J. remembers all the details."

"Yeah, sure. Go on now. Go someplace." Balzic went back to the radio console, shaking his head, sighing, swearing, asking himself what he'd done to deserve A.J. for a penance. Why A.J., he asked himself. Why not go to Rome and go across St. Peter's Square on my elbows and toes? . . .

He picked up the cards and dealt out another game of solitaire, then another, and another, losing thirty-some times before he quit counting. A few hands later, he stacked the deck, put it back in its box, and tried to tell himself he had been concentrating, which he knew was a ridiculous lie.

All the while he'd been playing, he had been worried by the idea that Frances Milocky wouldn't be able to tell them any more than they already knew. He was sure Keenan was right: Janet Pisula had not been doing her own work. He was just as sure that she had made a deal with somebody to do her work at Frances Milocky's insistence. He was equally sure that, unless they were dealing with a transient as Johnson had first worried about, unless Frances Milocky had a name for them, they'd be no further ahead than they were now. They'd have to run down every piddling, puzzling little note on every college bulletin board in three counties, all on the long chance that those notes were still available, all on the guess that the somebody who had written Janet Pisula's papers was the person who'd killed her, and all that on the even longer chance that that somebody advertised that way. Then there was the reason . . .

Suppose it had been that someone who had written her papers. Why would he kill her? Surely not because she owed him money. If it had been that, then why was there all that money in her desk and in her wallet?

And rape? Forget it. The girl still had her hymen. Sodomy? Nothing doing there either. Grimes's report made a point of noting the absence of sperm or semen anywhere in or on the body.

Which left the blank sheet of paper. And left Balzic with the idea he'd heard from Mo Valcanas: Hemingway blowing his head off because he couldn't make a sentence anymore. Was it that simple? Was that why a man killed himself? If that was so, would a man kill someone else because he couldn't make a sentence anymore? Balzic chewed his teeth. The whole idea, as simple as it had seemed when Valcanas explained it, now seemed as porous and fragile and mysterious as cobwebs.

Yet there had to be a parallel, something Balzic could understand, something he could reconcile himself to, and he fumed about the duty room, telling himself that if only he thought about it enough, he would find it. A half-hour later, he still had not got anywhere closer to the substance of the idea than he'd been when he put the cards away. He'd never felt more inadequate in his life.

The screen door jerked open, and Stramsky, swearing and scowling, came in and stood on the other side of the counter. He put his head in his hands and nearly shouted at Balzic. "Sometimes, Mario, my old lady makes me so fucking mad. She is so goddamn dumb sometimes. Most of the time she's okay, understand, but there are times, Jesus H. Kee-rist . . ."

Balzic started to smile and then to laugh.

"Hey, it's not funny, Mario."

"Vic, you're beautiful."

"What the hell are you talking about? Beautiful, Christ. My old lady just went out and made a deal to sell toys. So she can have Christmas money, she says. The only thing is she don't read the fine print in the contract she signs, and now she gives me the good news she got to come up with five hundred for her inventory. I say where the hell we gonna get five bills, and she says she already borrowed it from a finance company. I say how can you do that without my signing, and she tells me she forged my name. She does all this last week and just now she tells me about it, and you, you goddamn half-breed, you stand there laughing and telling me I'm beautiful. Jesus fuck!"

Balzic went through the lifting door and put his arm around Stramsky's shoulders. "Vic, Vic, I don't mean to laugh, honest to God I don't. And I can appreciate your situation—"

"You can, huh? You know what that fucking loan is going to cost us? That five bills is going to cost seven hundred and thirty-something by the time we get through paying it off. And you can *appreciate* my situation! I said, Jesus Christ, woman, there went all the profits you think you're going to make from those toys—that's if you sell them—and she says, oh no, I'll make a terrific profit. She thinks she's going to make so much money she's going to pay off that loan in twelve months. That's what she actually says to me. And you, you bastard, you *appreciate* my situation."

"I do, Vic, honest to Christ I do. It's just that I was sitting in here breaking my head trying to figure something out, and I couldn't, and you just walked in and laid it out for me. Believe me, I'm not laughing at you. I'm grateful. No shit, I am. And I'll tell you what. I'll call Mo Valcanas for you and ask him to get you out of it, how's that?"

"She signed, Mario! How's anybody going to get me out of it? She signed. The toy contract may be a hustle, but that don't cut nothing with the finance company. They don't care how you spent the money. You signed, you pay."

"Yes, but fraudulently, Vic. Fraudulently. She forged your name, right? Listen, if anybody knows how to get you out of this, it's Valcanas—that is, if you want out."

Stramsky hung his head. "Oh, Mario. You should've seen her face. She wants to do it so bad. How can I make her get out of it? She was so excited she was going to make some money by herself. This is the first time since we been married, you know? She never worked, you know that. And she really wants to do it. I almost got to admire her guts."

"Well, you do what you want, then let me know. You want out, I'll get Valcanas for you. If not, just say so, okay? Just believe me, I wasn't laughing at you."

"I believe you," Stramsky said. "I just hope it works out. You want to play some gin?"

"Not now. I'm going up to Troop A. I want to talk to Johnson and wait it out with him. They're picking up a girl I want to talk to. I'll give you a call later unless something comes up. Take it easy, Vic. It'll be all right," Balzic said, going out to his cruiser.

* * *

"We got her," Johnson said as Balzic walked into Troop A's duty room. "Picked her up in Blairsville. She should be here in thirty, thirty-five minutes."

"That's the second best news I heard today," Balzic said.

"Second best? Christ, what do you want? What was first?"

"Ah, I'll tell you after we hear what she has to say."

"Okay with me. You eat yet?"

Balzic shook his head.

"Let's go get one of those good antipastos Funari makes. He's still in business, isn't he?"

"Oh yeah."

"Still making those antipastos? It's too hot for anything else."

"They deliver now. We don't have to go."

"Nah, I want a couple beers too. Besides, I got to get out of this place for a while."

"Let's go then."

In Johnson's cruiser on the way, Johnson asked, "So what's this first best news you heard today?"

"One of my people's old lady got sucked into a toy-selling thing."

"That's good?"

"Good, bad, who knows. It really doesn't matter. What mattered was the way he looked and the way he was talking when he told me about it."

"He couldn't have looked too good."

"As a matter of fact, he looked mad enough to strangle her."

"You serious?"

"Yeah I'm serious. He wouldn't do it, but he looked like he wanted to. And that was the thing that's been bothering me about this Pisula girl. Why'd the guy do it, you know? That was really bugging me. He didn't rape her, he didn't rob her, so what's with him?"

"I figure he's a psycho, especially because of that paper."

"Yeah, but, Walk, nobody's just psycho. They're psycho for a reason. Lots of reasons. So he left a message, the paper. But why? I mean, I'm not saying I know, but at least now I think I got a start."

"Which is?"

"She was dumb."

Johnson mulled that over as he pulled into the parking lot of Funari's Bar and Restaurant. He looked at Balzic a few times but didn't say anything until they were inside at a table and taking sips of their first beers. Then, after the waitress had taken their food order, Johnson leaned over and said incredulously, "She was dumb?"

"Yeah, yeah, I know. It sounds ridiculous, but that's it. I mean, she was. Remember what her uncle told us? She went from skipping grades to barely keeping up. I got more or less the same story from all her teachers. Dumb—literally. Practically a mute. Which wasn't her fault, but that's the way she was. You can't get around that."

"And a guy kills her because she's dumb?"

"Yeah. He loses patience with her. He gets frustrated about something. I don't know what. But I'll bet it was something she wouldn't tell him. Wouldn't or couldn't, I don't know which."

"Then, just for the sake of argument, Mario, then what the hell was she doing with just her pants on? Why don't you think he killed her 'cause she wouldn't come across?"

"I don't know why I'm not thinking that way, but I'm not. Maybe it's because of the paper."

"You're thinking if he killed her because she wouldn't screw him, he would've just left, is that it?"

"I'm not sure," Balzic said. "But I think that's the way I'm thinking. I mean, that piece of paper took some thought. It isn't

141

something a guy in a panic does. If he's panicked, all he wants to do is get the hell out of there."

"Okay, then tie it up with her being dumb," Johnson said, screwing up his face.

"I don't know. Maybe he's telling the world she couldn't write. Maybe he thought that was something really terrible. If he's in the kind of business we think he's in, maybe he thought all his customers were extra stupid. Maybe they pissed him off. Christ, I've known more than one bartender who couldn't stand drunks. I even met a doctor once who really couldn't stand sick people. He said they were sick because they were all stupid and didn't take care of themselves. I'm not sure where I'm going with all this. All I'm saying is this is a start for a motive. Christ knows we got the body. But without a motive?" Balzic spread his arms wide.

"I don't know, Mario. You always were one for the psychology bit. Me, I just get them off the streets. Let the head-benders figure them out."

"Well, listen, Walk, look at it this way. How many times have you wanted to cream somebody for doing something stupid? One of your own people—how many times? How many times have I? How many times has anybody? Why do teachers paddle kids? Why do parents? What the hell business are we in, you and me?"

"Oh, come on, Mario. There's a hell of a difference between what's dumb and what's illegal."

The waitress brought the antipastos then and asked if they wanted more beer.

Johnson nodded to her, but Balzic just handed over his glass to her and demanded of Johnson: "Well? What's the difference?"

"To answer the thing about teachers and parents paddling kids, most teachers and parents I know don't really paddle kids for not being able to learn. They do it because the kids misbehave."

Balzic nodded vigorously. "Sure. That's what they say. But most misbehavior is nothing but kids doing what grownups think are dumb things."

"Not only dumb, Mario. Sometimes dangerous. To themselves as well as to other people."

"Yeah, but dangerous things are usually dumb things. Things that aren't good or sensible or reasonable or prudent. How many court decisions go with that one, that prudent?"

"A lot. No argument there."

"Well what's prudent mean? When a judge says a guy did not act in a prudent manner, what's he talking about? I mean, hey, when you get right down to it, if the guy was really prudent, how'd he get grabbed in the first place? What the hell, man, prisons are for screwups. People too dumb to not get caught."

"I think you're oversimplifying it."

"Tell me how."

"Right now I just want to eat. But don't let me stop you. Keep talking," Johnson said, biting into a ripe olive and chewing around the pit.

"Look," Balzic said, gesturing with a piece of Genoa salami, "right now there's a second-story guy I know, and I know he is. Christ, I've had him in so many line-ups in front of people who just caught a glimpse of him that he gives me the rag that I ought to put him on the force. His whole story is burglary, beginning to end. You know how many convictions? One. When he was eighteen. That's like ten years ago. He did six months in the workhouse in Allegheny County. Since then, nothing. The bastard's a pro. He works alone, he never looks the same way twice any two times I've had him picked up, he lives quiet—that fuckin' guy must've knocked over three hundred houses in the last ten years and nobody can come up' with even circumstantial on him. You know what he says? He says three things whenever I pick him up. He says, 'Hi, Chief,' 'When's the line-up?' and 'Can I go now?' The last time was the first time he ever said anything else. He said, 'Geez, I been in here so much, maybe you oughta give me a job.'

"Right now," Balzic went on, "there's a lot of noise in Harrisburg about no-fault car insurance, no-fault divorce, and what's the word they're kicking around about drugs? Decriminalizing, that's it. There's a lot of noise. Maybe these things will happen, maybe not. But as it stands now, practically everything is the adversary system. Somebody's at fault, and somebody got hurt, and whoevers at fault has got to give up some time or some money. At least in the civil system, whoever gets burned has a shot at compensation. In the criminal system, whoever gets hurt is supposed to be satisfied his taxes are keeping the criminal off the streets, which is supposed to deter others." Balzic snorted. "Deterring others, Christ. Some satisfaction that must be. I can see me running a gas station or a grocery and some junkie comes in, cleans out my register, and then blows it all on three fixes before he gets grabbed. Then I go give my testimony against him and watch him get one to three and five years pro. I keep on paying taxes to support the whole goddamn system, meantime I don't get my money back, the money the junkie copped in the first place. There's no provision for it."

"What's all this have to do with killing a girl because she was dumb?" Johnson said, smiling ironically at Balzic.

"Not a goddamn thing. You just said to keep talking. You wanted to eat."

"Well, it was a hell of a speech while it lasted. You sounded for a while there like you wanted to be a lawyer for the Chicago Seven."

"Oh boy," Balzic said, laughing, "you should've heard me

last winter when I talked to the Lions Club. Three or four guys walked out. You could've heard a flower hit the floor when I sat down, and the president of the club, Christ, he looked like he wished he'd shown a travelogue or something."

"What did you talk about?"

"More of the same I just gave you. You'd be surprised how little the squares want to hear how the criminal justice system really works. What they really want to know is what a good job I'm doing keeping the dopers and long-hairs out of their neighborhood."

"What kind of job are you doing?"

"Aw, shut up and eat, willya? Jesus."

Frances Milocky, disheveled from hours of riding, was waiting in the duty room when they got back to Troop A Barracks. She sat on the front edge of the chair, her face vacant, her left leg crossed over her right, her foot swinging, her fingers turning a pack of cigarettes end over end on her knee.

Johnson introduced himself and Balzic and then asked, "Do your parents know where you are?"

She nodded, her long, straight hair falling over her cheek. "I just called them," she said.

"Would you like some coffee? A Coke maybe?"

"Nothing, thank you."

"I think it would be better if we talked back in my office," Johnson said, leading the way back to it. "We won't have to put up with the radio."

The girl lifted herself out of the chair with great effort and followed Johnson with labored steps, her sandals sliding along the floor. Once inside Johnson's office, she slumped into the chair Balzic held for her.

"Miss Milocky," Johnson began, "I'm sure this isn't going to be pleasant for you, so if there's anything we can do to make it easier, just say the word, okay?"

She chewed her lower lip and nodded, turning the cigarette pack end over end against her knee as she'd been doing in the duty room.

"You ought to know, Miss Milocky," Johnson said, "that we've read the letters you wrote to Janet Pisula."

"I guessed that you did, otherwise you wouldn't want to talk to me. Of course, you could've heard about me from Uncle Mike. Janet's uncle I mean. He's not mine. I've just called him that for so long I sort of think of him as my uncle. Anyway, he would've told you about me."

"He did. But what we're really interested in is some of the things you wrote to Janet. You mention what seems to us—the chief here and myself—at least two men. One of them you named, and we know he was Janet's English teacher last year. Keenan."

"Yes," Frances said, nodding slowly. "Janet was terrified of him."

"Was there any particular reason?"

"You have to understand, lieutenant. Janet was afraid of all men. It didn't have anything to do with sex. Don't get that idea. It was because of the accident."

"Her uncle told us about that."

"Well, then you know. Then he must've told you about the man who caused the accident, the one who came to see her in the hospital."

"Yes, we know about him. The one who told her she should've died."

Frances nodded and pressed her fingers against her forehead. "Well, you must have figured out what that did to her."

"We have a pretty rough idea, yes. But we'd like to hear anything you can tell us."

She shook her head impatiently. "What can I tell you? It was traumatic, that's all. Not the kind of dopey little things people are always calling traumatic. That was a real trauma. It was a real wound. And it never healed. Someday maybe it might have. I mean, coming here to school, getting out of her house and on her own. Nobody will ever know what kind of courage that took. She went into a kind of frenzy whenever we'd be someplace and some young guys would want to talk to us. I could feel her shaking beside me. It was real hell for her to meet strangers. And if they were young guys, it was all she could do to keep from passing out, and I mean literally passing out."

"We gathered as much, but what in particular was there about Keenan? Or was there anything about him?"

"No. I don't think there was anything special about him except that he used to harp about the open admission policy the college had, and if there was anything particular, it had to be that. I mean, Janet had enough reason for feeling that she didn't belong. Anywhere. Not just in college."

"What's an open admission policy?" Balzic said.

"Anybody gets in who wants to. There aren't any prerequisites. As long as you have the tuition, you have to be admitted."

"And you advised her to transfer out of Keenan's class, is that it?" Johnson asked.

"Yes. She didn't have to listen to him. She'd been told once that she didn't belong. That once was enough for anybody, more than enough."

"You also advised her about something else," Balzic said.

"I was always advising Janet. I may be the world's greatest nonstop adviser. I know everything. Except it turns out I didn't know very much at all." Tears started to roll down her cheeks. She blinked a few times but didn't wipe them away.

"What didn't you know?" Balzic said.

"Oh God, what didn't I know! Everything. I didn't know how really terrible it must have been for her. And it was so easy for me to do cartwheels on the sidelines. A regular pom-pom girl of the mind, that's what I was. Bouncing up and down and yelling Janet locomotives."

"I'm sorry," Johnson said. "You just lost me."

"Oh, you must've seen football games. The cheerleaders spell out the name of their team. They yell a letter, the crowd yells the letter back."

"That's what you were for Janet?"

"That's what it turns out I was. Without intending it, but I must've really thought I knew what I was doing, I must've actually believed that all I had to do was cheer long enough and loud enough and Janet would just go out and beat her problem, as though it was a game or something. The really stupid thing is that I didn't realize it until I was on the bus."

"Where were you going?"

"I don't know. I really don't. All I could think of was I had to go somewhere. I just couldn't stay around and face Uncle Mike, even though I knew he wouldn't think I was responsible. But I felt I was. And I felt so stupid. The worst was that my major is psychology. And I went to Penn State actually thinking I was already a clinical psychologist because of the miracle I'd performed on Janet. All I had to do was get the degrees. What did anybody really have to teach me? My God, I'd guided a practically autistic girl into emotional stability just by cheering . . ." She broke down completely then, sobbing into her hands and swaying on the edge of the chair.

Minutes passed before she got control of herself and when she did, she said, "I never thought how cruel and mean good intentions can be. The best intentions. I've heard that platitude about history being bloody with good intentions, or however it goes. I can't even think of it now. But I never thought for a minute I could ever be stupid enough to be one of those people, those super sentimental creeps who think they have all the answers and really believe they know what's best for other people. But, well, here I am." She tried to smile but had to bite her lower lip to keep it from trembling.

"Uh, Frances," Balzic said, "did you advise Janet to get somebody to do her work for her, to write her papers—"

"Yes," she interrupted him. "You have to understand. All Janet wanted to be was a secretary. She didn't want to be a reporter or a novelist or a poet or any other kind of writer. Janet wasn't stupid. She was slow—what other people would call slow—because she had a hard time articulating her thoughts because for a long time everything she thought was so terrible, she just refused to talk about what she was thinking. Then, when she finally did start to talk, she went through a period when she questioned everything, when unless she had a completely satisfactory answer for why she was doing something, she just wouldn't do it. Then, when she started to talk with me pretty easily about what she was thinking I persuaded her to write everything down so we could talk about it—oh, God, she was my project. I had all these methods, these asinine therapeutic methods. . . ."

"I know this is tough for you, Frances," Balzic said, "but you're thinking about yourself now and, uh, you're feeling a little too sorry for you now and you're not doing us much good."

"I know, but I have to give you some background, otherwise you won't understand why I told Janet to pay somebody to write her papers for her."

"Okay," Balzic said, "tell it the way you want."

She took a deep breath. "Okay. Well, Janet started to write everything down and then we'd talk about it. Her dreams, her questions, her reactions to things that happened to her. They were really amazing things. She had a really terrific insight into herself. That's why I never believed she was badly injured in the accident, or if she was injured, brain damaged, then all it did was bring her down to my level. Not in school. In school she just barely got passing grades, but that wasn't because she couldn't do the work. She'd get sidetracked. She was always questioning why she was doing something. She never took anything for granted. Not the simplest things.

"Like once," she went on, "she was supposed to write a term paper, a research paper with at least ten references in the bibliography, an outline, footnotes, the whole bit. But she never did any research at all—not in the library. She wrote the whole paper on the act of writing. The whole paper was a description of her hand and a pen and the movements and thought which directed the movements. Her teacher didn't know how to react to it—or to Janet. She gave Janet a D because she said Janet just didn't do the assignment. And that's why she had trouble in school. She did exceptional work, only it was never what she'd been assigned to do, and then when the teachers called her in to talk about it, Janet wouldn't say anything to defend what she'd done."

"Is that what happened in Keenan's class?" Balzic said.

"That's exactly what happened."

"So you told her to get somebody to do the papers for her."

"I had to. Because if she went on the way she was, she was going to flunk and I knew she'd just get the guilties over spending her uncle's money and disappointing him—which he wouldn't have been—but that didn't matter to her. It was a choice I really forced on her. I mean, I knew if she paid somebody to do the papers, she'd pass, and then she could get on with what she really wanted to be good at: typing, shorthand, bookkeeping.

That was really all she wanted to be. A secretary. And it isn't any great mystery why. She understood it very well."

"Not that there's anything wrong with that, but why did she?" Johnson asked.

"She wanted to get a strange man's approval. She was absolutely honest about it. She used to say that just once in her life she wanted to have the confidence in a few skills so she could ask a strange man for a job and he would give it to her and then he would have to give her raises because of her competence. She never wanted anything to be given to her that she didn't deserve, but she desperately wanted approval from a man she didn't know."

"I don't get that," Balzic said. "Didn't she see Keenan as a strange man? I mean, why wouldn't she try to get his approval? Why didn't she try to write papers that would suit him?"

"In Janet's mind, getting a grade from a teacher wasn't approval. That was just a grade. Approval to her meant getting money to live on. Earning her way was the same in her mind as life itself, especially if the money came from a stranger. Do you see what I mean? I mean, being a good secretary, getting a job from a stranger, being competent, gaining the stranger's approval, all that would have wiped out what that other man said. The one who killed her mother and father and told her she should've died. It may not sound logical to you, but it is psychologically sound, and it was how Janet interpreted her life."

"She had this all figured out?" Balzic asked.

"Oh, yes. She was completely honest about it."

"Then why did you put her in a position where she'd have to be dishonest?" Johnson asked. "I mean, that's what it looks like you did to me."

Frances hung her head. "I know it sounds like that, but what else could I tell her to do? If she kept up the way she was going, she'd get hung up on something that was very important to her but didn't have anything to do with the assignment. And then she wouldn't have been able to become what she wanted. That's why she had the most trouble in English classes. All through school. As long as it was grammar, she was fine. But when she had to write something, when she saw that blank sheet of paper in front of her, she was just overwhelmed by the possibilities of what she could put on it."

Balzic and Johnson exchanged surprised frowns.

"Would you say that again?" Johnson said.

"What?"

"What you said about the blank sheet of paper and the possibilities."

"Well, I don't know how to say it any differently. She'd look at the paper and she'd say something like, 'I can put anything here I want.' And then she'd say, 'Now what do I want here? There are thousands of words I could use. Which ones do I really want here?' That's the way she used-to talk about it."

"So you told her to get somebody who was all business, is that it? Somebody who'd get the assignment from her and wouldn't get hung up. He'd just get right to it," Balzic said.

"Yes. Otherwise, she'd spend hours picking the first word."

"Well," Johnson said, "that leaves only one thing. Do you know who that person was?"

"I don't know him, no. I arranged it through a girl Janet and I knew who went to Pitt in Oakland. I'll have to think a minute to remember his name. It was unusual. I mean I thought it was unusual because his first name was Italian but his last name was Slavic. Serbian or Croatian probably."

"You could be talking about the chief here," Johnson said, smiling vaguely at Balzic. "He's got an Italian first name. Mario. What was your father, Mario? Serbian?"

"Yeah," Balzic said, rubbing his mouth and chin. Then he

canted his head and said to Frances, "Wait a minute. That guy's name wasn't Anthony, was it?"

"Yes, that's it. Anthony—oh, it starts with an S."

"Segalovich?"

"Yes, that's it. How did you know?"

"How did I know, huh? How did I know." Balzic was snorting and fumbling for his notebook. "I had him, right in my lap I had him and was too dumb not to put two with two." He found the Keenans' phone number and address and dialed the phone on Johnson's desk.

"Mario, what're you talking about?"

"I had him. This afternoon at Keenan's house. He was who they were arguing about. Didn't I tell you about him?"

"No," Johnson said.

"I had to tell you. That's how I found out about the paper-writing hustle."

"You told me Keenan's wife told you."

"Yeah, but she told me 'cause I was curious about him. I wanted to know how he made his living. How do you like those potatoes, huh? Right in my mitts I had him. And boy, do things start to fall into place now—hello, Mrs. Keenan? This is Mario Balzic, the chief of—"

"I remember, chief. Can I help you?"

"I hope so, Mrs. Keenan. You remember that guy who was at your house this afternoon?"

"I can't very well not remember him."

"Yeah, well I know you said you weren't sure where he lived, but maybe your husband can, and I'd—"

"That person—for want of a better word—is here right now. Do you wish to speak with him?"

"He's there now?"

"I'm sorry to say he is."

"Terrific. You just keep him there. I'll be right down to take him off your hands."

"Chief, you, uh, sound a little ominous. I might even say a little frightening."

"It's nothing for you to worry about, Mrs. Keenan. I'll be there in a couple minutes." Balzic hung up and headed for the door, tearing the page with the Keenans' address out of his notebook and giving it to Johnson. "Come on, Walk. I'll go sit on him and you go get a warrant. And oh, Frances, you do us a favor and see if you can locate your friend, the one who arranged for Segalovich to write Janet's papers, okay? And when you get her, you tell her to sit tight. We're going to need her, okay?"

Frances nodded slowly, her face slack with remorse, bewilderment, betrayal. . . .

Mrs. Keenan was pacing in the kitchen when Balzic knocked on the screen door. She was startled by the sound and stood very still in the middle of the room. "Is that you, chief?"

"Yeah, it's me. All right if I let myself in?"

"Please do. I'm shaking so much I don't think I could open the door."

Balzic let himself in quietly and said, "Is he still here?"

She nodded once. "Chief, I'm scared to death. I really am."

"You got no problems. There won't be no hassle, believe me."

"You don't understand. I know why you're here, but something happened while I was talking to you on the phone—I mean, I think I can guess why you're here. To arrest Segalovich?" She was talking just above a whisper.

"Yeah, but nothing's going to happen to you—"

"That's not what I mean. While I was talking to you, Mal came out to the kitchen and he—he got some grass, some marijuana. They smoked it in Mal's study and I . . ."

"They're stoned? Both of them?"

"They were having a giggling fit when I last saw them. But I haven't heard anything for a while."

"Well, that'll make things easy."

"Easy?" Mrs. Keenan looked unbelieving.

"Sure. Potheads are the easiest collar—arrest, I mean. They just get nervous in the car. They always complain I'm driving too fast. They see a red light, they start hollering for me to stop a block away from it. I get a kick out of them, to tell the truth. They really make me laugh."

"Yes, but my husband, I mean, isn't possession a felony?"

"Mrs. Keenan, I could care less what your husband's holding. I want Segalovich. If you're worried about your husband, forget it. I should thank him for putting Segalovich in the shape he's in. Hell, now I can sit down and wait until the warrant gets here. If you don't mind."

"Please do."

Balzic settled onto a stool and lit a cigarette. "Mrs. Keenan, when I talked to you this afternoon, I asked you how long Segalovich had been here, and you weren't too sure. Try to think now, will you please? And put your feelings about him aside. I know that part's tough, but try to remember exactly when he showed up."

Before she could answer the sound of heavy, unsteady footsteps came to them, and then Malcolm Keenan appeared from around the corner. His eyes were red and wet, and he was having trouble trying not to giggle.

"Did I hear someone say when was the last time they showed off?"

"No, Mal, you did not. You most certainly did not hear that."

Keenan ignored his wife and tried to focus on Balzic. "You look similar, sir. Are you an original or are you a copy? Have you been . . . where was I?" Keenan started to rumble with giggles. "I remember not, I mean I remember now. Similar, Similac. Baby food. You're a diaper salesman."

Balzic laughed and said to Mrs. Keenan, "See what I mean? They're really funny."

"I am not amused," she said.

"No, no," Keenan said. "It's we are not amused. We. Not us. Not I. We are not . . . what aren't we?" He shook with giggles again.

"Amused," his wife said, "and if you could get yourself together you wouldn't be either."

"Wouldn't be what?"

"Oh Mal, for God's sake!"

"God," Keenan said. "Theism, I-ism, you-ism, we-ism, they-ism."

"Will you stop your word games just once! Just this once," Mrs. Keenan said, dropping her head and covering her ears with her hands.

"Women," Keenan said, grinning lopsidedly at Balzic. "Woman is a contraction of woe and man. And you can spell it either way; you can spell it *w, o, e,* or *w, h, o, a.* Sorrow and stop. That's women, or whatever . . ."

"Mal, your fellow free spirit, your poet in my residence, the one you always told to test the depths of his loathing, the one you encouraged to despise you, that same person may very well have found the depths of his loathing—do you understand me? Mal? Answer me."

"I would if I could but I can't seem to want to," Keenan said. "I'm trying to make some other association that is very important. Aha! This man is not a diaper salesman."

"Bravo, Mal. That he is not. He is a policeman. The chief of police, and unless I'm mistaken, another policeman is on his way here with a warrant to arrest your friend."

"Aaaaah, yes. The fuzzz. The fuzz with Roethke in his note-book. The commissar cum dilettante, the better to know me. And one can spell that *k, n, o, w,* or *n, o.* Either way, he is here to know me or no me . . ."

"Not you, Mal. Segalovich. Your friend is suspected of killing that girl."

"Really? I mean, really? That's, oh my . . . I'm afraid my toes are sending me messages. They say the world is spinning very fast and that gravity is very grave . . ."

"Damn you, Mal. Damn you!" Mrs. Keenan wheeled out of the kitchen. Her footsteps could be heard going through the house and then up some stairs. A door slammed overhead.

Keenan shrugged wearily at the sound, then turned to Balzic. "Did I hear her correctly? Or did I miss something?" He giggled. "Do you know what I almost said? I almost said, 'Did I thing some miss,' but I knew that would never do . . . oh, Shazam, Shazam, why don't I ever turn into Captain Marvel?"

"I give up," Balzic said, laughing, "why don't you?"

Keenan took a very deep breath, then another, and said, "I have no idea . . . say, did you say you suspect someone?"

"If I didn't, then your wife did."

"Who? And of what?"

"Anthony Segalovich. Murder."

"Are you serious? Murrr-der. That's impossible. Don't you see, I mean, can't you see—a poet who's in shape is never accused of rape."

"Yeah, well, that might be, but I didn't say anything about rape. I said murder."

"You yes—I mean, yes, but you see, it follows that if he's in shape and he's never accused of rape, why then he would never conceive of murder . . . where was I?"

"You're still right here, Mr. Keenan."

"*Doctor* Keenan. I have not been a mister for some months, or is it years? No matter . . . excuse me, but don't you think it would be wise to discuss this with Tony? I mean, but you should talk with him."

"Okay," Balzic said, standing. "Let's go discuss it with him. Where is he?"

"Follow me," Keenan said, gesturing dramatically, sweeping his arm in a great arc which came to a painful stop when his hand slammed into the refrigerator.

"You sure you can get us there?"

"Certainly," Keenan said, grimacing and opening and closing his hand and wiggling his fingers. He weaved around the corner and led Balzic through a formal, almost Victorian dining room, past a flight of carpeted stairs, and into a cluttered room with a desk, on which sat an old, office-size typewriter, heaps of papers, magazines, and books. Books were stacked haphazardly on a set of shelves which leaned precariously away from one wall, and there were more books stacked on the floor near the desk. There were two chairs, one a Boston rocker, the other a large wooden chair of indistinguishable manufacture, and a short couch.

On the couch, sitting with his shoulders slumped, his large hands hanging between his knees, his head tilted to the left, his eyes wide and red, sat Anthony Segalovich breathing deeply and slowly. His mouth curved up to the right in a half-smile. Without looking at either Keenan or Balzic, he said, "Man, am I skyed. This stuff is wow. Super wow." He made a faint whistle and let his head roll slowly to the right.

"Tony, it's the fuzz," Keenan said, settling uneasily into the Boston rocker.

"You ain't shittin' it's the was," Segalovich said.

"No, no, Tony. Not was. Fuzz."

"Fuzz, was. Was fuzzy. Was fuzzy ever wasy . . ."

Balzic lit a cigarette and looked around for an ashtray. He found one on a small table beside the Boston rocker and balanced it on his knee as he sat in the wooden chair.

"What're you smokin', man?" Segalovich said, focusing momentarily on Balzic.

"Tobacco."

"Ouu, that's bad for you. You can get cancer and every . . . wow, you should've felt that one. That one, that was like, wow, like nuclear . . . hey, man, tobacco's bad. You can get strokes, heart attacks, cancer. You can get cancer of the ass . . . you gotta shit through a hose into a bag and everything . . . hey, Mal, didn't I tell you?"

"Tell me what?"

"What what?"

"What didn't you tell me?"

"I forget," Segalovich said, smiling and rolling his head slowly while staring at something on the braided rug.

"Segalovich," Balzic said, "I guess it's about time I informed you of your constitutional rights."

"Consti-what? Man, I haven't shit in over a week. All I do is throw up."

"No," Balzic said, laughing. "Constitutional rights. Try to read my lips. Con-sti-tu-tion-al rights."

"Oh, them. Yeah, I got them. I got them all over the place. I can pray anywhere I want. I can assemble. I can even reassemble. I can do a whole bunch of stuff, man. I can even speech. Guaranteed."

"Yeah, well that's close but not close enough. So try to pay attention."

"Oh no. Nothin' doin'. I'm not standin' up for nobody. Are you kiddin', man? I'm nailed to this, whatever this is." Segalovich pounded the couch with the flat of his hand.

"Then try listening carefully."

"Oh yeah. I can do that. Go ahead. Listen something at me and see if I do it carefully. I bet I can do it, man."

"Okay," Balzic said, "in a little while, a state police lieutenant will be here with a warrant for your arrest. The charge—"

"I'm with you so far, man. And carefully, too. Don't forget that, man. Carefully."

"Yeah, I've noticed that," Balzic said. "The charge will be murder."

"Murder? Phew, that's a baaaad rap. That's almost badder than gettin' busted for dealin'."

"A little worse, I think."

"Well, 'sa difference of opinion. So go 'head."

"You have the right to remain silent."

"Silent, man. Wow, that's really, you know, like quiet."

"You have the right to legal counsel, and if you don't know any or can't get one, it's the obligation of the Commonwealth to provide you with one."

"Hey, that's pretty nice of them, you know? You know that, Mal? I mean, providin' me with all that."

"Only if you're unable or unwilling to get one by yourself."

"Hey, like right now, I don't feel like gettin' one, you know? I mean, I couldn't even find the phone right now, you know? I mean, my ass is really tacked to this thing here. I mean, stapled, man."

"Yeah," Balzic said, "I know what you mean."

"Well, my arse is not stapled," Keenan said, getting wobbily to his feet. "And I will call one for you, Tony. The best one I know."

"Hey, that's really nice of you, Mal. I mean, no shit. It really is."

"*De nada,*" Keenan said, weaving around Balzic and out of the room.

"Okay, so he's going to call a lawyer for you," Balzic said, "but

I want you to understand, clearly understand, that anything you say between now and the time the lawyer gets where you are—anything at all—will be used against you in a trial. Do you understand what I just said?"

"Yeah, man, I can understand that. But do you understand that I'm fuckin' skyed? I'm like up there with the seven-forty-sevens, man."

"That doesn't mean a thing. It doesn't make a bit of difference to a court. Booze, grass—a court doesn't care if it's marshmallows. All I got to testify to is that you said you understood me when I told you your rights. So just between you and me, I wouldn't say anything if I were you. I'd just sit there and enjoy that stuff until the lawyer shows."

"Man, you don't understand," Segalovich said, giggling. "I got nothing to hide. My life's an open book. It's a lousy book. Corny characters, stale plot, bad dialogue, no style, no nothing, but it's open. Just like a shithouse in a state park or someplace. I mean, you *know* people been shittin' there before you. You can smell their stories, man, so you don't sit all the way down. You just sort of go into a crouch and let her plop." Segalovich giggled again. "That is, if you ain't constituted, you can go plop. But if you're constituted, well, tough shit." Segalovich rocked with silent laughter, and then doubled over, rolling back and forth on the couch.

Balzic continued to sit and smoke, watching Segalovich as he sat upright finally, his eyes wet and red, his diaphragm heaving, his face slack. He sat like that for a minute or so, smiling vaguely at some sensation from the marijuana, rolling his head ever so slightly from side to side. Occasionally, he would throw his shoulders back, take a deep breath, and expel it audibly.

"You know," Segalovich said, looking at the floor, "you can never really control anything . . . you can try. You can really break your ass and your brain trying, but you can never really get anything under the kind of control you think you ought to have . . . you know what the fuck I'm talkin' about?"

"I think so," Balzic said.

"I mean, all the time I spent in the gyms, man, all those hours and weeks and years. All that time, man, on the side horse, on the high bar, the parallel bars, vaulting, working on the free exercise, working the still rings . . . all those hours. All those exercises, all those weights I lifted, all those isometrics I did . . . all that to control my body, man. And for what? All because my old man almost made somebody's Olympic team about a thousand years ago . . .

"Ain't that something? I mean, really. All that to learn control, to learn when to get your hips under, your legs together, your toes pointed, the exact moment when to take off and when to start your shoulder turning . . . all that because a guy I can't even remember used to do it. All that because the broad he married, the one he screwed to pop me out, all that because she thought I should do it because he would've wanted me to do it . . .

"And you know, for a long time, man, I really believed I should be doing it because I really believed in it. I mean to tell you, man, I really ate that crap up, just scarfed it up. I thought, yeah, baby, this is really where it's at, this is really the way to control things, really control things. Get so good at those things, man, you could make your body do damn near anything. And all the while, man, it wasn't my life. I was doing it and really diggin' it and really bein' good at it, and I wasn't in control of nothing. No, man. It was my old lady was in control. All the time. She was in charge of my whole life . . .

"I'd be in a meet, man, and there she'd be. She wouldn't have to tell me she was going to be there, man. I could feel her there.

I swear she breathed different, and I could hear her breathing in the stands. And when I'd fuck up, when I'd miss a move, start it too soon or come off it a fraction too late, I could hear her breathing change.

"And then she'd start to shout, man, and carry on. She'd start shouting, encouraging me. A one-woman cheering section. The better I got, the louder she got . . . and then she'd start anticipating me, man. Yelling at me when to start my next move, what to look out for, what mistakes I could make . . . it was fuckin' embarrassin', man . . .

"That last time, what a circus . . . it was an AAU meet, and I was on the rings. There was, like, two events to go, and I'm so far out front in points, I'd have to break a leg to lose, you know? But I got started wrong on those fuckin' rings. Man, those fuckers just started swayin', man, and I couldn't get them stopped. A foot in each direction, and I just could not get those bastards still . . .

"I was going to go from a handstand right into an iron cross, two strength moves in a row. Lots of points . . . but goin' into the handstand I almost went over the top and the goddamn rings were swayin' worse than ever. I mean, I was having a real bitch holding two seconds up there. It was like two minutes . . .

"And I came down too fast. My feet went way out in front. Christ, I arched my back so hard I pulled something in it, just trying to keep my ass under . . . I go into the cross, and the place is quiet, man, the way it always gets when people see somebody goin' wrong. They get quiet, man, 'cause they're really watchin' to see if the guy can pull it off. And there I am, swayin' like I'm on a fuckin' trapeze, countin' the seconds—you got to hold it for three—and my old . . ." Segalovich started to laugh hard so that it became difficult for him to talk. ". . . and my old lady is down out of the stands, man, and she's praying. Praying, man.

She's saying, 'God, don't sway. God, please don't sway. Please, God, don't sway.' And you know what?"

"No, what?" Balzic said.

"I felt like I got hit by lightning, man. I mean it. Like fucking lightning. There I was, two seconds into the iron cross, waiting for the third second to pass, gruntin' my ass off, goin' nuts 'cause I can't get those rings still, and there's my old lady, praying. It was the sequence that got me, man. First it was, 'God, don't sway.' Then it was, 'God, please don't sway.' And then the clincher: 'Please, God, don't sway.'

"And there it was, man. In the third second, it hit me. Like lightning, I knew, man. I knew! I mean, it was so fuckin' corny, but it was perfect. You can't write that kind of stuff, man. You can't make a story out of it. You can't make poetry out of it. It's too fuckin' corny. I mean, there I was, man, crucified doin' an iron cross, and there was my old lady down there prayin' for me, prayin' *to* me, man, to satisfy somebody I didn't even know who was God around our house . . . like lightning, man, I was Jesus. I mean, I wasn't, but I was! I actually knew what it felt like to be up on that cross waitin' to die, man, listening to the women prayin' for him to be what nobody can ever be. What nobody can be, man. Nobody."

"What's that?"

"Perfect, man. Nobody can be that. I mean, I know what a perfect performance on the rings might look like. Might. But nobody ever does it. Nobody ever has and nobody ever will . . . but there was my old lady down there, tryin' her ass-off to turn me into the son of God . . . 'Please, God, don't sway' . . . and all because that bastard was dead and I was all she had. . . ."

"What did you do?"

"I just started to cry, man. Just bawl. And then I just dropped down out of the cross, man, and I started to swing, back and forth, just like kids do in a park. I was swingin' so hard, I was fuckin' near goin' over the top. And then I started to laugh . . . you should've seen the people, man. They were goin' bananas trying to figure out how to get me down off those rings. The judges, man, the coaches, they were all running around like wild, man. And my old lady, she's screamin' at me. 'Please, God, Anthony, stop it.' Over and over and over. Christ, it was funny. . . ."

"How did they stop you?"

"I don't know. Next thing I knew I was in a hospital somewhere, Pittsburgh, I think. I don't even know. They had me so fogged up with Thorazine, man, I didn't know what my name was. . . ."

Keenan came in then and said, "Attorney Louis Margolis will be here within the hour. He advised me to advise you, Tony, to say absolutely nothing until he arrives."

Segalovich listened to Keenan and then shook his head and laughed. "Hey, Mal, no shit. How come everything you say got to sound like the Gettysburg Address? I mean, really, man, all you need's a beard and a top hat."

"What do you mean by that?" Keenan said.

"What do you mean by that?" Segalovich mimicked him. "Now what the shit do you think I mean? Everything you say, man, you say like you're running for Congress. That's the way you sound, man. Like you're giving a position paper or a news conference or some goddamn thing. Like everything you say is going into a briefcase which is gonna get handcuffed to somebody's wrist and wind up in Istanbul or Helsinki or some fucking place."

Keenan took several very deep breaths and squared his shoulders. "In view of the fact that I have taken it upon myself to obtain counsel for you, Tony, and especially in view of the seriousness of the charge against you, I think it's about time you began to take an altogether different attitude—"

"There you go again, man. Another fuckin' speech."

"As I was saying, I think it's about time you began to assume the attitude apropos the situation, which attitude it seems would be one of the most practical realism."

"Oh, I am, man, I am. I have never had a more realistic attitude than I have right now. I mean, I've leveled off, man. Super Jay, the joyous Jamaican, has got me up to twenty-seven thousand feet, and I'm locked into automatic pilot. I got time to look around and survey the crew, see if everybody's in order, and, man, you're as out of order as anybody I've ever seen. And the reason you're so out of order is 'cause you spend your whole life trying to get out of order. Man, you're the only guy I know who's made a career out of being disorderly in an orderly way. You're full of shit, man, precisely because you got diarrhea, if you know what I mean." Segalovich started to laugh, but his face was no longer slack and his eyes no longer vague. Either the marijuana was starting to wear off or else he had reached an interval of lucidity on his way to another of giggling, seemingly disjointed indifference.

Keenan, for his part, was standing as though prepared for military inspection. His chest was out, his heels together, his thumbs resting on the seams of his trousers. "This is not the time for acrimony," he said solemnly. "You are in serious trouble. I am befriending you. This is not, most definitely not, the time for acrimony."

"Aw, for crissake, man, sit down," Segalovich said. "You keep standing there like that, you're gonna rupture yourself or something . . . 'not the time for acrimony,' Jesus. Befriending me, shit. All you ever did was finish the job my old lady started, you know that? Between the two of you, my old lady and you,

you two fuckers got me crazy . . . she wants to turn me into a chimpanzee, and you want to turn me into a chimpanzee that can type . . . still rings and sestinas, the horizontal bar and heroic couplets, the side horse and satire, free exercise and free verse . . . is it any fuckin' wonder I'm doing giant swings inside my head? And all the time tryin' to figure out how I'm goin' to dismount? I should've killed you two . . . what the fuck'd I have to kill her for? Come on, Doctor motherfuckin' Keenan, tell me why. You're so goddamn full of announcements, pronouncements, affirmations . . . 'The universe announces yes, who am I to profane the universe by announcing any less,'—ain't that your fuckin' story, Doctor Keenan? What the hell are you a doctor of anyway? Doctor of Philosophy, shit. Doctor of sick ideas, is that what you are? Tell me something, doctor of sick ideas—d'you ever cure one yet?"

"Tony," Keenan said evenly, "I would advise you to say no more. I am advising you of this because if you continue to speak as you are, you will only succeed in getting into greater difficulty than you are."

"Greater difficulty than I am?" Segalovich howled with laughter. "Man, how much difficulty could I be in! You don't understand nothing, man. Nothing! I could split your head open with an ax and pour in some real information, only you got so much shit backed up in there, none of it would filter through. The joke is, we're the same, you and me. I'm constipated in my ass, you're constipated in your brain. You haven't had a new idea since Christ was a carpenter. The bigger joke is you know it. You've known it all along. That's why you're a fucking poet, man, instead of a man who writes poetry. Any asshole can be a poet. *Be* one. But write it? Uh-uh, no way. Man, that takes work. You got to sit down at the machine and get the words on the page, man. Anybody can walk around makin' fuckin' announcements he's a poet. But when you sit down at the machine and look at that blank page, man, that's like standing under those goddamn rings, waiting for somebody to lift you up so you can take hold and do it, man. *Do* it!

"All the talk in the world about keeping those rings still won't keep them still. Just like all your bullshit about being a poet don't get any words on the page . . .

"And I believed you! I actually believed you . . . this is all a bad joke, man. One box inside another box. I believed my old lady, my old lady believed in my old man, she believed in me, I believed in you. And you—you told me I could be a poet. I should've known right then from the way you said it. I could *be* a poet, you said. Shit, man, I can't even write a simple goddamn story. First this happened and then that happened. I can't even do that. Now go ahead, ask me how I know I can't. Go ahead. Either one of you. How about you, cop? You probably the only one really wants to know anyway. The doctor of sick ideas here wouldn't understand."

"How do you know?" Balzic said.

"Because I tried, man. Because I tried over and over and over. And you know whose story I was tryin' to write?"

"Janet Pisula's?" Balzic said.

"See there, Keenan? The cop knows more than you ever will." Tears filled Segalovich's eyes. "The cop knows, and you know what he knows? He knows I couldn't even tell how a girl got so scared of living she wanted to die. You know how many different ways I wrote her story, man? I lost count, that's how many. Because no matter which way I wrote it, it came out wrong. All it was words. All words, just words . . .

"And you know what finally came to me? There was nothin' but words on those pages about her because there was nothing in me to put on those fuckin' pages. All I knew was she was like me. Something got in her head that somebody else put there.

She didn't have a life. She'd been dead for years. All I did was make her stop breathing. . . ."

"Is that why you went there?" Balzic asked.

"Hell no. I went there to get some bread she owed me."

"But we found a lot of money in the room."

"Hey, you just asked me why I went there and I told you. I didn't say anything about taking any money. When it hit me, I mean, when I saw it . . . shit, money was the last thing in the world that made any difference. What good was fifteen bucks going to do me? What good is fifteen thousand going to do me right now? Fifteen million . . . man, you only need money when you got some tomorrows coming. . . ."

"You didn't even ask for the money, did you?"

Segalovich shook his head. "What for? I wanted to see what was inside her—can you understand that? That's what I really went there for. I wanted to find out how come she was dead. So I could write it, man. I mean, when somebody's dead and they're still walking around, it's a goddamn story, you know? But how the fuck do you find out?"

"You might've tried talking," Balzic said.

"Goddammit, man, that broad never talked! She never said one more word than she had to, and half the time you couldn't hear that." Segalovich heaved his shoulders in a deep sigh. "When I used to go there to do her papers for her, she'd have the assignment written down, and she'd just hand it to me. Then I'd sit down and write it and I'd try to show her what I was doing, you know? So she might learn a little something for herself, you know? But I never knew whether anything I said was getting through."

Balzic thought for a moment. "Is that—that last time—is that what made you try to make love to her?"

"You're too much, man, you know that? Too much,"

Segalovich said, shaking his head. "How did you think of that?"

"Well, it looked pretty obvious. She didn't have anything on except her panties. There wasn't any struggle. You had to've at least started with that in mind."

Segalovich's shoulders sagged. "Yeah, that's the way it started out. For the dumbest-ass reason in the world. I went in my head from trying to get inside her head to find out why she was dead to getting in her to see if maybe she was still alive and I was too dumb and too blind not to see it. I thought maybe I could feel it. Like, shit, I don't know, like maybe my body could feel something my head couldn't think. I mean, hell, there was a time when I could make my body do damn near anything. Maybe it could even think. . . ."

"But it didn't work," Balzic said.

Segalovich gave a snorting, self-deprecating laugh. "That's got to be the all-time understatement of the world, man. The alltimer to end all-timers. 'Cause that's when I found out I was dead, man. I couldn't feel a thing. All the while she was undressing, man, I couldn't feel a single motherfuckin' thing. All I remember is I started to shake. Just shake all over. And then that fuckin' line of Roethke's Keenan is always quoting jumped at me. 'This shaking keeps me steady. I should know.' That jumped at me and it had a hammer in both hands. It just started pounding on my head . . . I could hear Keenan, just like he was there, reciting it . . . and then my mother was breathing funny in the stands, I could hear her like she was there. And there was this broad right in front of me, this dead broad with her nipples as round as round could be, and all I could think of was those fuckin' rings, and, man, so help me, that brassiere was the same color, the exact same goddamn color as the gloves I used to wear . . .

"The next thing I knew she was saying something about I was him. She just kept saying it, over and over. 'You're him, you're him, you're him,' and I was asking her, who am I? Who am I supposed to be? But all she said was the same thing, over and over. And I knew it was important. I mean, really important. Like if she'd only tell me, then maybe I could go somewhere and write her story and get it right and get it out of me. But I couldn't get it out of her. She wouldn't say who I was or who he was or why I was him . . .

"And then, my head just zipped out on me. Zip-zip, gone. And there she was, man . . . all I did was lay her down real easy, like, as though, like I was trying not to hurt her. Can you imagine that? I just strangled the fuckin' broad and I'm laying her down easy 'cause I don't want to hurt her. . . ."

"What did you do then?" Balzic asked.

Segalovich shook his head. "I don't know. I can't remember a thing. Nothing. All I know is I was here, heaving my guts out in the bathroom upstairs."

"You don't remember how you got here?"

"Nothing. I don't remember how or when or why. I was just there one minute and the next minute I was here, that's all."

"What about the paper?"

"What about the what?"

"The paper. That blank sheet of paper."

"Man, I don't know what you're talking about."

"There was a blank sheet of paper on her stomach. You had to put it there."

"Man, I'm telling you, the last thing I remember doing was laying her down real easy. That paper you're talking about, I don't know anything about any paper. And I'll tell you straight, man, this fuckin' Jamaican, you cops ought to use it. If it gets everybody else the way it gets me, you guys ought to find out about it, 'cause I can't lie when I got this shit in me. I see the lies startin' in the back of my head and runnin' around and gettin' close to my tongue and then I just see them goin' back where they started from.

"Like a minute ago, one started. I was going to tell one about how it's everybody else's fault that I killed that girl, Keenan's, my old lady's, my old man's, everybody's. It was one of those lies some jackoff Ph.D. in sociology or psychology would've come up with. Like I didn't have any choice. Like given the givens, man, somebody like me would just naturally wind up killing somebody . . . statistical determination. Freudian determination. Calvinistic determination, whatever the fuck you want to call it. But that was a bullshit lie, man. I killed that girl all by myself. I killed her 'cause she was me. 'Cause I didn't have the fuckin' guts to kill myself . . .

"And you know what she said, man? Right when I was doing it? She said, 'Please.' Yeah. Not, 'Please don't.' No. She said, 'Please.' . . . poor, dumb fuckin' broad. She couldn't write either. . . ."

Segalovich stood then, momentarily lost his balance, but steadied himself by holding onto the arm of the couch for a few seconds. He straightened slowly and said, "Come on, cop. Take me wherever the fuck you're gonna take me. I stay here any more, I'm going to throw up all over Keenan's typewriter, and he wouldn't appreciate that. I mean, he'd say throwin' up was also part of the affirmation of the universe, but I still think it'd piss him off."

Balzic stood and started to lead Segalovich out of the room, but stopped short of the doorway and said to Keenan, "Listen, when that lawyer gets here, you tell him we'll be at Troop A Barracks and we'll wait for him so he can be at the arraignment, okay?"

Keenan seemed not to hear.

"Uh, Dr. Keenan, d'you hear what I just said?"

"I'm sorry. I was—I was. Yes, I was, that's what I was."

"Yeah, well, did you hear what I said about the lawyer and where we'll be?"

"Yes, I heard. It just took a moment. I was thinking of something."

Segalovich faced Keenan. There were tears in his eyes. "Mal, I hope you do think of something, man. I really do." Then he turned to Balzic and said, "Let's go, okay? Only one thing."

"What's that?"

"No handcuffs, okay? I couldn't stand that. I couldn't stand to have those things on me, you know?"

"I know," Balzic said, leading him through the house and onto the porch where they met Johnson coming up the steps.

"This him?" Johnson asked.

Balzic nodded. "Keenan called a lawyer for him, and I told Keenan to tell the lawyer we'd wait for him up at your place."

"You mean we're not going to have him alone?"

"We don't need to, Walk. Not that way. He'll tell you everything you want to know. Maybe a couple things you don't want to know."

"He confess?"

Balzic nodded. He was going to say something, but was interrupted by Segalovich's laughter.

"What's funny?"

"I was just thinking, man," Segalovich said. "The first thing I want you to know, it's not funny. I'm just laughing 'cause I don't feel like crying. But what I was thinking about was my old lady got a scrapbook about this big." He held his hands about three inches apart. "Filled with pictures and clippings, all about me. I was just wondering if she was gonna cut this out of the paper

K.C. CONSTANTINE

too, you know? I mean, she was always saying she was saving the last couple pages for when I finally made it, whatever the fuck she thought that would take. But what I was laughing about, man, all of a sudden it just came to me. I mean, now I know why they call them scrapbooks, you know?"

"Yeah," Balzic said, "I see what you mean."

Johnson took hold of Segalovich's elbow and led him down the steps and to his cruiser. Just before he opened the door, he called back to Balzic, "You coming?"

"Nah. I'll catch you in about a half-hour or so. I got to go talk to my wife."

"Something wrong?"

"Not yet," Balzic said, going to his own cruiser, "but there's going to be if I don't go talk to her. I got to tell her her brother's turning into a dirty old man and I don't want him around my daughters. I been putting it off for a couple years, but right now I suddenly got the feeling this is the time to say it."

"Well, if that's what you have to do," Johnson said, shrugging.

"It is," Balzic said, getting into his cruiser and turning the ignition. He watched Johnson drive off, then turned around in the alley behind the Keenans' house and headed for home.

He found Ruth in the kitchen and he told her as gently, as kindly as he could what was bothering him about her brother. Though it settled nothing about their spending a weekend in her brother's cottage, and though much of what he said made Ruth angry, he was glad he had not wasted any more time figuring the right way to say it. In the morning, he was very glad for that.

174

ABOUT THE AUTHOR

Carl Constantine Kosak (1934–2023), better known as acclaimed mystery writer K.C. Constantine, is famed for his mysteries featuring Mario Balzic. Constantine showed much more interest in the characters in his novels than the actual mystery, and his later novels became ever more philosophical, threatening to leave the mystery genre behind completely. In 1989, Constantine was nominated for the Edgar Allan Poe Award for Best Novel for *Joey's Case*. Despite his success, he managed to keep his literary identity completely hidden until 2011 when he appeared in person for the first time at the annual Festival of Mystery hosted by Mystery Lovers Bookshop in Oakmont.

THE MARIO BALZIC MYSTERIES

FROM MYSTERIOUSPRESS.COM
AND OPEN ROAD MEDIA

MYSTERIOUSPRESS.COM

Otto Penzler, owner of the Mysterious Bookshop in Manhattan, founded the Mysterious Press in 1975. Penzler quickly became known for his outstanding selection of mystery, crime, and suspense books, both from his imprint and in his store. The imprint was devoted to printing the best books in these genres, using fine paper and top dust-jacket artists, as well as offering many limited, signed editions.

Now the Mysterious Press has gone digital, publishing ebooks through **MysteriousPress.com**.

MysteriousPress.com offers readers essential noir and suspense fiction, hard-boiled crime novels, and the latest thrillers from both debut authors and mystery masters. Discover classics and new voices, all from one legendary source.

FIND OUT MORE AT

WWW.MYSTERIOUSPRESS.COM

FOLLOW US:

@emysteries and Facebook.com/MysteriousPressCom

MysteriousPress.com is one of a select group of publishing partners of Open Road Integrated Media, Inc.

THE MYSTERIOUS BOOKSHOP, founded in 1979, is located in Manhattan's Tribeca neighborhood. It is the oldest and largest mystery-specialty bookstore in America.

The shop stocks the finest selection of new mystery hardcovers, paperbacks, and periodicals. It also features a superb collection of signed modern first editions, rare and collectable works, and Sherlock Holmes titles. The bookshop issues a free monthly newsletter highlighting its book clubs, new releases, events, and recently acquired books.

58 Warren Street
info@mysteriousbookshop.com
(212) 587-1011
Monday through Saturday
11:00 a.m. to 7:00 p.m.

FIND OUT MORE AT:

www.mysteriousbookshop.com

FOLLOW US:

@TheMysterious and Facebook.com/MysteriousBookshop

OPEN ROAD

INTEGRATED MEDIA

Find a full list of our authors and
titles at www.openroadmedia.com

FOLLOW US
@OpenRoadMedia